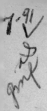

W9-AEC-450

At sixteen and a half, Lady Imeldra is ready to leave
school and resume a carefree life with Earl Kingsclere,
her father. But the Earl has other plans for Imeldra
who rebels at being sent to live with her strict grandmother. She runs off to the estate of Marizon where
she loses her heart to a brooding, cynical Marquis—
and determines to free him from a blackmailing
Frenchwoman and win his love!

LOVE AND THE MARQUIS

A Camfield Romance

Dearest Reader,

This is a new and exciting concept of Jove, who are bringing out my new novels under the name of Camfield Romances.

Camfield Place is my home in Hertfordshire, England, which originally existed in 1275, but was rebuilt in 1867 by the grandfather of Beatrix Potter.

It was here in this lovely house, with the best view in the county, that she wrote *The Tale of Peter Rabbit*. Mr. McGregor's garden is exactly as she described it. The door in the wall that the fat little rabbit could not squeeze underneath and the goldfish pool where the white cat sat twitching its tail are still there.

I had Camfield Place blessed when I came here in 1950 and was so happy with my husband until he died, and now with my children and grandchildren, that I know that the atmosphere is filled with love and we have all been very lucky.

It is easy here to write of love and that is why I feel you will enjoy the new Camfield Romances which come to you with *my love*.

Bless you,

Books by Barbara Cartland

THE ADVENTURER
AGAIN THIS RAPTURE
ARMOUR AGAINST
    LOVE
THE AUDACIOUS
    ADVENTURESS
BARBARA CARTLAND'S
    BOOK OF BEAUTY
    AND HEALTH
THE BITTER WINDS OF
    LOVE
BLUE HEATHER
BROKEN BARRIERS
THE CAPTIVE HEART
THE COIN OF LOVE
THE COMPLACENT WIFE
COUNT THE STARS
CUPID RIDES PILLION
DANCE ON MY HEART
DESIRE OF THE HEART
DESPERATE DEFIANCE
THE DREAM WITHIN
A DUEL OF HEARTS
ELIZABETH EMPRESS OF
    AUSTRIA
ELIZABETHAN LOVER
THE ENCHANTED
    MOMENT
THE ENCHANTED
    WALTZ
THE ENCHANTING EVIL
ESCAPE FROM PASSION
FOR ALL ETERNITY
A GHOST IN MONTE
    CARLO
THE GOLDEN GONDOLA
A HALO FOR THE DEVIL
A HAZARD OF HEARTS
A HEART IS BROKEN
THE HEART OF THE
    CLAN
THE HIDDEN EVIL
THE HIDDEN HEART
THE HORIZONS OF LOVE
AN INNOCENT IN
    MAYFAIR

IN THE ARMS OF LOVE
THE IRRESISTIBLE BUCK
JOSEPHINE EMPRESS OF
    FRANCE
THE KISS OF PARIS
THE KISS OF THE DEVIL
A KISS OF SILK
THE KNAVE OF HEARTS
THE LEAPING FLAME
A LIGHT TO THE HEART
LIGHTS OF LOVE
THE LITTLE PRETENDER
LOST ENCHANTMENT
LOST LOVE
LOVE AND LINDA
LOVE AT FORTY
LOVE FORBIDDEN
LOVE HOLDS THE
    CARDS
LOVE IN HIDING
LOVE IN PITY
LOVE IS AN EAGLE
LOVE IS CONTRABAND
LOVE IS DANGEROUS
LOVE IS MINE
LOVE IS THE ENEMY
LOVE ME FOREVER
LOVE ON THE RUN
LOVE TO THE RESCUE
LOVE UNDER FIRE
THE MAGIC OF HONEY
MESSENGER OF LOVE
METTERNICH: THE
    PASSIONATE
    DIPLOMAT
MONEY, MAGIC AND
    MARRIAGE
NO HEART IS FREE
THE ODIOUS DUKE
OPEN WINGS
OUT OF REACH
THE PASSIONATE
    PILGRIM
THE PRETTY
    HORSE-BREAKERS
THE PRICE IS LOVE

A RAINBOW TO HEAVEN
THE RELUCTANT BRIDE
THE RUNAWAY HEART
THE SCANDALOUS LIFE
    OF KING CAROL
THE SECRET FEAR
THE SMUGGLED HEART
A SONG OF LOVE
STARS IN MY HEART
STOLEN HALO
SWEET ADVENTURE
SWEET ENCHANTRESS
SWEET PUNISHMENT
THEFT OF A HEART
THE THIEF OF LOVE
THIS TIME IT'S LOVE
TOUCH A STAR
TOWARDS THE STARS
THE UNKNOWN HEART
THE UNPREDICTABLE
    BRIDE
A VIRGIN IN PARIS
WE DANCED ALL NIGHT
WHERE IS LOVE?
THE WINGS OF ECSTASY
THE WINGS OF LOVE
WINGS ON MY HEART
WOMAN, THE ENIGMA

Camfield Romances

THE POOR GOVERNESS
WINGED VICTORY
LUCKY IN LOVE
LOVE AND THE MARQUIS

A Camfield Romance by

BARBARA CARTLAND

LOVE AND THE MARQUIS

A JOVE BOOK

LOVE AND THE MARQUIS

A Jove Book / published by arrangement with
the author

PRINTING HISTORY
Jove edition / August 1982

ISBN: 0-515-06295-2

Jove books are published by Jove Publications, Inc.,
200 Madison Avenue, New York, N.Y. 10016. The words
"A JOVE BOOK" and the "J" with sunburst are trademarks
belonging to Jove Publications, Inc.

PRINTED IN THE UNITED STATES OF AMERICA

Author's Note

Citrus trees were cultivated by the Hebrews from about 500 B.C. There is a talmudic legend that the citron was the fruit Eve offered to Adam in the Garden of Eden.

The word for 'citrus' in modern Hebrew is *hadar*. It is used in Leviticus 23 : 40 to describe 'the fruit of a goodly tree' which grew in the Garden of Eden, the so-called Tree of Knowledge.

The 'bitter orange' was brought from the East by the Arabs and the Moors cultivated it in Spain. In England Orangeries became fashionable in the early sixteenth century and many great architects of the eighteenth century were commissioned to design them.

The Regency architect Humphrey Repton first designed top-lighting and also added the Orangery or Conservatory to the house.

The greatest difficulty in growing citrus fruit was heating. Queen Henrietta Maria's Orangery in 1649 was lined with mattresses and reeds. An Orangery at Ham House in Richmond used heat from a laundry arranged in the same building to warm the plants.

There are very fine Orangeries at Warwick Castle (erected in 1780), at Burleigh House, first designed for Queen Elizabeth I's Lord Chamberlain in 1561 and replaced 200 years later by 'Capability' Brown, and the largest and most magnificent at Morgan Park, Swansea built in 1790.

chapter one

1833

THE Earl of Kingsclere walked restlessly about the very impressive Salon, not noticing the magnificent pictures, the china which in itself was worth a fortune, or the array of hot-house flowers which decorated every table.

There was a frown between his eyes and the lines on his handsome face which had beguiled so many women were sharply etched.

He was worried and it showed in every movement he made, in every breath he drew.

He walked to the grog-tray in a corner, which one would not have expected to find in such a very feminine room, and poured himself out a glass of champagne.

He drank deeply as if he was in need of it, and

then with what appeared almost a reckless gesture he raised his glass and said aloud:

"To the future!"

As his voice echoed round the room the door opened and the Butler announced:

"Lady Imeldra, M'Lord!"

The Earl started and stared incredulously as a young girl, for she was no more, came running down the room towards him to fling her arms around his neck.

"Papa! I was so afraid that you might be away when I arrived!"

"Imeldra!" the Earl exclaimed. "What are you doing here? I was not expecting you."

"I know that, Papa. I have run away!"

Her arms tightened round him and she kissed her father on either cheek so that it was impossible to answer her.

Then he put his hands on her shoulders to hold her away from him so that he could scrutinise her.

"You are lovely!" he said. "Far lovelier than I expected you to be."

"Oh, darling Papa, I did so hope you would think so."

"You are very like your mother," the Earl said in a low voice, almost as if he spoke to himself. "And she was the loveliest woman I have ever seen."

Imeldra would have kissed him again, but he held her firmly from him saying:

"You have a lot of explaining to do. Why have you run away from School?"

"To see you!"

The Earl's eyes twinkled.

"I do not believe that is the only reason."

"Actually it is not," Imeldra replied. "I was in trouble and I suspect they will sack me anyway."

The Earl laughed as if he could not help it.

"That sounds more like the truth. Now come and tell me all about it. Would you like a glass of champagne to sustain you?"

"May I really have one?"

"I imagine you are old enough now and when you arrived I was just drinking a toast to the future."

She looked at him questioningly.

"That sounds very unlike you, Papa, and I have never known you to drink when you are alone."

The Earl did not answer. He merely poured her out a very small amount of champagne and filled his own glass.

Then he walked to the window where the pale early April sunshine was just percolating through the clouds. Then he sat down.

There were two chairs and as Imeldra sat down opposite him his eyes were on her hair, appreciating that the sun picked out the red lights amongst the gold.

He gave a deep sigh.

"You are beautiful, which is what I hoped you would be."

It was not a compliment. He was merely stating a fact, that Imeldra's eyes seemed to hold the light in them as if somebody had lit a candle within her.

They were very unusual eyes, large, liquid, and their depth seemed to hold a mystery which the Earl knew would make a man look and look again, as he attempted to solve the secret that lay hidden in them.

Then as if he forced himself to be practical he said:

"Now tell me why you are here."

"Do you know how old I am, Papa?"

"Not old enough to leave School."

"But I am! And it is humiliating to be the oldest pupil by several months!"

"Is that true?" the Earl enquired.

"I promise you it is and honestly, Papa, I can learn no more there."

She gave him a quick glance as if she expected him to argue with her, and when he did not she went on:

"I am the Head girl! I am top in every subject, and it was really embarrassing last Speech Day when I won almost every prize. Finally I am not prepared to spend the Easter holidays alone."

"Alone?" the Earl asked sharply.

"Oh, Papa, you must remember that Schools have holidays! All the girls are going home next week, except for me."

"But I thought something was always arranged for you in the holidays."

"I have been fortunate that one of my friends has always invited me home with her, but now I have no invitations."

"Why not?" the Earl asked mystified.

Imeldra's eyes twinkled as his had done and there was a mischievous smile on her lips as she asked:

"Why do you think?"

"If I said what is in my mind, it would make you very conceited."

"Yes, that is the reason. I am too pretty! My friends are grown up, and they dislike seeing the young men who they think are courting them transferring their attention to me."

"I suppose it is understandable," the Earl murmured.

"Of course it is, dearest Papa. I am your daughter, and . . . Mama's."

Imeldra's voice softened as she spoke of her mother and she was almost sure she caught a look of sadness in her father's expression before he said:

"I am beginning to understand your reasons for leaving, Imeldra, but your decision to run away could not have come at a worse moment."

"Why?"

For a moment the Earl seemed to feel for words. Then he said almost recklessly:

"Because I am doing exactly the same thing!"

Imeldra sat bolt upright.

"Oh, no, Papa, not again?"

"I do not know what you mean by that," her father said. "This is different."

"Dearest Papa, you know as well as I do that each new love affair of yours always seems different, until you grow bored."

The Earl rose to his feet as if it was impossible to sit still and he walked across the room and back again before he said:

"All right, Imeldra, I am in a mess, and there is nothing I can do about it. So there is no use in your arguing with me."

"I would not do that. But I realise now that I should never have left you."

"Of course you had to leave me," the Earl said.

5

"You were too old to live the life I was leading. Now I think of it, it is a good thing that I am going abroad."

"Going abroad?"

"Tomorrow."

"And . . . who is going with . . . you?"

It seemed for a moment as if the Earl was reluctant to answer truthfully, then he said:

"Lady Bullington!"

Imeldra thought for a moment before she answered:

"I have read about her in the newspapers. She is very beautiful."

"Very!" the Earl agreed dryly.

"But, Papa, how can you be so foolish as to run away with her?"

"Lord Bullington intends to divorce her, and so I have to do the gentlemanly thing and give her my name."

"But that will take years, Papa. It always does."

"I know, I know!" the Earl said testily. "But we are going to live in Venice where I have bought a Palazzo."

"How lovely! That is something I have always wanted you to have."

"But you know," the Earl went on as if she had not spoken, "that you cannot come there until I am married, and even then it would be best if you stayed away."

Imeldra was silent, but he saw the hurt expression in her eyes, and he sat down again to say:

"Dearest child, you have to be sensible about this. When I sent you to School I told you, and you seemed to understand, that I could not allow my way of life," enjoyable though it might have been from my point of view, to spoil yours."

"We had such fun together, Papa," Imeldra said. "It has been ghastly without you these two years, but I believed...as you promised...that I could come back to...you once I was...educated."

"If you remember," the Earl contradicted, "what I promised was that when you were old enough, you should be presented to Society and I would do everything to see you accepted as your mother was when she was your age."

"But I did not think that I would not be with...you."

"You know perfectly well that the hostesses who would welcome you would not entertain me," the Earl said.

"There are plenty of other people who would," Imeldra insisted stubbornly.

"Not the sort of people that I want you to meet, not the sort of people of whom your mother would approve and, more important, not the sort of people where you will meet the sort of man I want you to marry."

Imeldra was silent.

She knew that the reason why, two years ago, her father had sent her away from him to School was that he had found her struggling in the arms of a young nobleman who was trying to kiss her.

The Earl had knocked him out. Then before he could recover consciousness he had thrown him bodily down the steps of the Chateau in which they were living in France, and told the servants never to admit him again.

But Imeldra, as her father realised, was growing up.

Nearly sixteen, she was no longer a child and it was a mistake for her to associate with his friends, either male or female.

She had therefore come to School in England, and because she loved her father she had agreed to work hard and try to become, in his words, 'a perfect Lady.'

But she had counted the days until she could be with him again and had no idea of his social ambitions for her, which would mean permanent exile from the one person she loved more than anybody else in the world.

Now her eyes filled with tears as she said in a broken little voice:

"Oh, Papa...how can...you be so...cruel to...me?"

"I know that is how it seems, my precious one," the Earl answered, "but it is because I love you, because amongst my treasures you are the most perfect of them all, that I cannot have you soiled and damaged by the life I lead."

"I love your life, Papa! It has always been such fun moving about the world with you, meeting so many different people, some of whom I admit were very strange and some very charming and unusual."

"Those sorts of friends are perfectly all right for a man," the Earl said, "and if you had been a boy, it would not have mattered in the slightest if you had what is known as a 'cosmopolitan education.' But for a girl it is disastrous."

"Why? Why?" Imeldra asked.

"Because, my dearest, you have to marry, and if

you think I want you married to one of the riff-raff
who will not only fall in love with you but be well
aware that I am a rich man, you are very much mistaken!"

"I have no intention of marrying anybody at the
moment."

"Every woman should marry," the Earl said
sharply, "especially somebody as beautiful as you.
You need a man to look after you and protect you,
but the sort of gentleman I want as a son-in-law is not
to be found at parties I give. If he is, he will not treat
you with respect."

"Why not?" Imeldra asked.

"Because, my darling, you cannot touch pitch and
not be defiled, and a man of aristocratic birth, especially an Englishman, wants his wife to be pure and
untouched, and certainly not to have had a 'cosmopolitan education.'"

Imeldra laughed because the way her father spoke
sounded so funny. At the same time, she knew that
in a way he was speaking the truth.

When she had last been with him she had become
aware for the first time that, although she was dressed
as a young girl and her hair was loose over her shoulders, the expression in men's eyes was different from
what it had been before, and they no longer treated
her as a child.

Aloud she said:

"I cannot lose you, Papa! You know you are the
only person to whom I belong."

"That is not true," the Earl answered. "You have
a great number of relations and I have already been
in communication with them. I have in fact, arranged

9

that your Aunt Lucy will present you at Court."

Imeldra looked at him wide eyed.

"The Duchess?" she exclaimed. "But I thought she never spoke to you."

"She loved your mother, and I have promised her that I will not interfere or even see you as long as you are under her chaperonage."

"Papa! How could you promise anything so... horrible... and so... cruel to... me?"

"And to me," the Earl added quietly. "But, my dearest, it is best for you."

Imeldra rose to stand at the window and looked with unseeing eyes out into the garden.

The daffodils were coming into bloom and the first buds were appearing on the trees, but she was thinking that she had only seen her aunt, the Duchess, once at her mother's Funeral.

She had seemed an austere woman, cold and controlled, who looked at everybody else as if they were beneath her condescension.

At the same time, Imeldra was intelligent enough to know that under the Duchess's patronage she would be accepted everywhere in the Social World that her father thought so necessary to her.

She knew too that the Duchess was a Lady-of-the-Bedchamber to Queen Adelaide.

She was also aware that while her father's raffish reputation as a roué had been easily acceptable during the reign of George IV, King William and his prim little German wife had changed the whole attitude of Society towards morality.

This meant that the Earl, whose amorous indiscretions had been admired and envied by the Georgian Bucks and Beaux, now evoked upraised hands and gasps of horror from those who wished to ingratiate themselves at Court.

Because the Earl was so handsome, and because, as Imeldra knew, women gravitated towards him like rats to the Pied Piper, he was always engaged in one love affair after another.

It was what prevented him from mourning the one woman in his life he had really loved—her mother.

He was also a sportsman, and his race-horses romped home regularly to take the most treasured prizes of the Turf.

He had, when he was younger, been an acknowledged pugilist and a champion swordsman.

Men admired, envied and fêted him, but those of them who prized their wives kept them away from a man who was too fascinating to be anything but a danger.

After her mother's death, when she had gone everywhere with her father, Imeldra had noticed the gleam that came into many women's eyes the moment they saw him.

She knew that long before he was aware of them they were yearning after him in a manner which she found sometimes amusing, sometimes irritating.

"I want to see Papa," she had said once to one of her Governesses who kept her in the School-Room when she had wished to go downstairs.

"Then you will have to wait your turn," the Governess had answered somewhat brusquely.

The only consolation was that her father grew very

quickly bored in every love affair, and his invariable habit when this happened was to move somewhere else.

Imeldra could remember when they had packed up and left a Palace he had rented in Rome at only twenty-four hours' notice because the dark-eyed and passionate beauty who had been constantly with them had suddenly become no longer welcome.

Her father in leaving so precipitately avoided the floods of tears and recriminations that inevitably followed one of his swift changes of mood.

He and Imeldra had journeyed to Greece, but while the Acropolis and Delphi had entranced Imeldra, her father's dalliance with a Maid of Athens did not last much longer than Lord Byron's, and they had moved on.

Egypt had been a wonderful place for Imeldra because her father found no modern 'Cleopatra' there and the women depicted on the Temple walls were very much more attractive than those who lived and breathed.

The Earl was a very well-educated man, and Imeldra had often thought recently that she had learnt so much more from him than from her teachers and books at School.

Yet because it pleased him she had worked at her lessons until, as she had said, she was top in everything, and there was really nothing more they could teach her.

She had been so sure that she would be with her father at least for a little time that she could hardly believe now that she was to be separated from him and the mere idea of it made her want to cry.

The Earl disliked tears, having endured too many of them from the women he had loved and left.

So Imeldra bit her lips to stop herself from sobbing and said in a voice that only trembled a little:

"Can I not...stay with you for...just a...little time...Papa? I have dreamt of you and...longed to be with...you and to...talk to you."

"That was what I too wanted," the Earl answered, "but because I have been a fool, Imeldra, it is now impossible."

"Must you...really run...away with...this lady?"

"It is something I have to do," he replied, "and you must expect me, as your father, to do the honourable thing."

"Not if you do not love her."

"Love? What is love?"

Then as he saw the expression on his daughter's face he said in a very different voice:

"You know as well as I do that I have only loved once in my life, and that sort of love never comes again."

"Is that true of everybody, Papa? That they love only one person with a real love which is what you had for Mama?"

"It was the way I loved your mother, and she loved me," the Earl replied, "and because we were the other part of each other, it would be impossible for any other woman to mean the same to me."

He spoke simply and to Imeldra his words were very moving.

"At the same time," he said as if he must tell the truth, "you know there have been times when I have been infatuated, beguiled and bemused by other women, but because I have known the highest and the best, I am not prepared to accept second best in my heart, whatever my lips may say."

"I understand, Papa," Imeldra answered, "and I hope that one day I shall love in the same way."

"That is the whole point," the Earl said as if she had played into his hands. "That is what I want for you, and that is what I am determined, if it is possible, you shall find."

Imeldra did not speak and he went on:

"But as I have already said, you will not find it in the gutters or in the sort of places where I reign as King, albeit over a very scruffy little Kingdom."

He laughed, but the sound had very little humour in it.

"Yes, a King, because I am rich, and because in a foreign land I am accepted by the noblest families who excuse anything I do since I am an English Milord!

"But you, dearest child, are not concerned with the French, the Italians, the Austrians or the Spanish, but with English Ladies. Their society is the most snobbish and the most critical in the whole world."

"Then why must I mix with them?"

"Because, my precious, only from the heights to which they can take you will you marry into the life that I wish you to lead, and meet the right sort of man who will offer you marriage."

There was a sudden sharpening of the Earl's voice as he went on:

"Make no mistake, from now on you will find it a great handicap that I should be your father. At the same time your beauty, your wealth and the fact that your aunt is a Duchess of impeccable respectability will make you acceptable."

"But, Papa, do you imagine I would agree to marry any man who thought of me in those terms?"

The Earl's voice softened and he said:

"He will also love you, my darling, love you passionately and with his whole heart. But his mind and his critical sense must assure him that in making you his wife he is doing the right thing."

Because Imeldra was perceptive and so closely attuned to her father, she knew exactly what he was trying to say to her.

She would have been very stupid if she had not been aware that many of the people he entertained in foreign Capitals would not have been acceptable in the aristocratic houses of England when ladies were present.

There had often been times when she had been told not to come downstairs, and she had known the following morning that the party that went on until dawn had been rowdy and very far from respectable.

She accepted it because she loved her father and because her life with him was so adventurous, delightful and constantly changing.

She had never known from one day to the next what would happen and often, when the lessons at School seemed extremely dull, she had slipped away back into the past.

When the class was droning over French irregular verbs, she could see in front of her eyes the beauty of Versailles, the clouds over Mount Vesuvius, the Coliseum or the crowds at St. Peter's when she was learning Italian.

When the teacher pointed to Greece on the map she saw the Acropolis and the ruins of Delphi.

"I am so lucky to have seen the real thing," she told herself.

She knew the other pupils in the class could not understand the beauty of such places that had become a part of her, something she could never lose.

The Butler announced luncheon and while she and her father ate they talked of the places they had visited in the past, and he told her about the Palazzo he had bought in Venice, which was a very old one.

As she had never visited Venice and could not visualise what he was trying to tell her, she said:

"Please send me a painting of it, Papa, so that I shall be able to feel that I am near you."

"I will do that," the Earl promised, "but even if we do not see each other, my dearest, we can still keep in touch by letter."

"And in our thoughts," Imeldra added. "I have often thought at night when I have been at School that I was sending my thoughts winging towards you, and wherever you were you would receive them."

"I am sure I did," the Earl replied, "and I am telling you the truth when I say that I was often conscious of your presence and my thoughts were continually with you."

"I think I know that, Papa, so you see, we can never really lose each other."

"No, of course not," the Earl said, but his eyes were sad.

As they walked back to the Salon Imeldra asked:

"When are you leaving?"

"I was intending to do so this afternoon," he said, "but I have changed my plans. It will not matter if

I reach London tomorrow morning instead of tonight."

"Then I can dine with you?" Imeldra asked in a rapt little voice.

"Of course!" the Earl agreed. "And we must also, my darling, make plans about where you are to go until your aunt is prepared to receive you."

Imeldra looked at him and he said:

"I happen to know from reading the Court page of *The Times* that she is in Scotland at the moment staying with the Duke and Duchess of Buccleuch."

"Good!" Imeldra exclaimed. "That means I cannot go to her until she comes South."

"Exactly!" the Earl said dryly. "Therefore, as you cannot return to School, you must go to your grandmother's."

"Oh, no, Papa!"

She was not at all fond of her grandmother who was old and at times very disagreeable.

She disapproved of the deep affection Imeldra had for her father, and had always resented that her granddaughter had not been sent to live with her as soon as her mother died.

There was no doubt, however, Imeldra knew, that her grandmother would welcome her as a guest.

At the same time she would not lose the opportunity of finding fault with the way she had been brought up, and Imeldra felt that to have to listen to endless diatribes against her father would be unbearable.

"Please, Papa," she pleaded, "do not send me to Grandmama's."

"Where else can you go, dearest, at a moment's notice?" the Earl asked. "You can drive there in the carriage in three to four hours."

Imeldra knew that was true.

"I will send my mother a letter," the Earl said, "explaining, for she will undoubtedly learn sooner or later the reason why I am leaving for France and shutting up the house."

Imeldra gave a little murmur of distress, but she did not speak and the Earl went on:

"Dutton will be in charge of everything. You can tell him to do anything you want."

Imeldra looked around the Salon.

She had not spent much time since her mother died at Kingsclere, which was the family seat. Before that it had been their permanent home.

It was only after his wife's death that the Earl felt that the place was haunted by the woman he had loved so deeply and he could not bear to be there without her.

It was then that with his small daughter he had set off on their travels to foreign lands.

Once or twice a year they came home and the Earl would run his horses at Ascot and at Newmarket.

He would be in the Jockey Club or the Royal Enclosure with some beautiful woman who had taken his fancy at that particular moment, while Imeldra, properly escorted, was allowed to roam amongst the crowds.

The Gypsies would tell her fortune, and because she was so pretty and so well dressed they were always very glamorous forecasts.

She would watch the Shysters and the Bookies and those who made their living by entertaining the crowds and extracting pennies from their pockets by doing so.

It had all been immense fun, and the summers at

Kingsclere were as vivid and as beautiful in her mind as anything she saw abroad.

But inevitably the end of the summer meant the end of the Earl's latest *affaire de coeur*.

As soon as he had shot the first partridges he would be off to the sun from the Mediterranean to North Africa, and once unforgettably, down the Red Sea to India.

It was a strange and varied life for any child, but Imeldra grew to girlhood with a wider knowledge than any of her contemporaries had, not only of countries and places, but of people with strange religions and conflicting political ideas.

Because her father was so intelligent, he spent his time not only with beautiful women, but with the Statesmen of the countries they visited, the Prime Ministers, the Chancellors, the Foreign Secretaries.

And when he entertained, Imeldra would listen to what they were saying and try to understand so that she could discuss it with him afterwards.

As they talked together after dinner that evening she had the feeling that no man she would meet in Society would ever be able to take his place, since even if he loved her their brains would not match each other's.

What was more, she would never be able to learn from him as she had learnt from her father.

Inexorably the evening came to an end, and when Imeldra looked reluctantly at the clock over the mantelpiece the Earl said:

"I am going to say goodbye to you now, my precious daughter. You know I cannot bear emotional farewells, so I am asking you, my darling, not to come downstairs until I have left tomorrow morning, which will be very early."

With an almost superhuman effort Imeldra bit back the words of protest that came to her lips.

She knew her father was right in that they had nothing more to say to each other, but when she saw him drive away she would want to cry because he would be going out of her life for a very long time.

She was aware that he was really saying to her that it would be a mistake for them to meet again until she was married.

The idea of losing him as well as having to marry somebody because he considered it the 'right thing to do' was terrifying.

However there was no point in saying so, and it would only make him unhappy. She could already feel the misery she would know once he had gone surging over her.

Instead she put her arms around his neck saying as she did so:

"I love you, Papa, and nobody in the whole world could have a kinder, more wonderful or more handsome father than I have."

"But not a very good one, I am afraid, my precious."

"That is where you are wrong," Imeldra said. "You have not only given me a wonderful childhood, but you have also given me high ideals and aspirations."

The Earl looked at her to see if she was telling the truth, and she said:

"Because we have always talked over things so sensibly, I am not bemused or fascinated by the things that are wrong. I merely accept them as part of living.

But you have always pointed out to me the things that are right and good and noble. And because you have always wanted me to aim for them, that is what I intend to do."

The Earl put his arms around her and held her very close to him.

"Thank you for saying that to me, my sweet," he said. "It makes me very happy. I have often been afraid that your mother was reproaching me because I had not let you be brought up by your grandmother."

"Mama would have understood that I had to be with you," Imeldra said. "And because I know what you meant to each other, I also know exactly what I want to find in a husband."

Because the Earl could find no words in which to answer, he merely kissed her. Then he said:

"If things go wrong, if you are in trouble, you have only to send for me, and you know I will come to you from the very ends of the earth."

"Just as I will come to you, Papa, if you want me."

Her father kissed her again, and as if there was nothing more they could add to what they had already said to each other, with their arms linked they walked up the great staircase to where they were sleeping in bedrooms adjacent to each other.

The Earl kissed her again on both cheeks, on her eyes, and her forehead.

Then without saying anything he went from her bedroom and closed the door.

For a moment Imeldra thought she must throw herself down on the bed and let the tears that were pricking her eyes become a tempest of weeping.

Instead she went down on her knees to pray to her

mother to protect her father and keep him from coming to any harm.

It was a long time before Imeldra went to sleep, and when she awoke early the next morning it was to hear movements outside in the passage and to know that her father was leaving.

It was then that once again the misery of being without him seeped over her and it was only thanks to years of exerting self-control that she prevented herself from rushing out and holding onto him and begging him to take her with him.

Then she remembered that that was the sort of thing that the women who had loved him and with whom he had grown bored would have done, and she refused to lower herself to be like them.

Instead she put her hands over her ears and stopped herself from hearing him go.

Only when she was quite certain he had driven away in his smart Phaeton drawn by four horses did she take her hands away and lie back against the pillows, feeling as if she was exhausted by the conflict within her.

Finding it impossible to stay in bed, she got up and dressed without ringing for the housemaid and went downstairs.

Everything in the house looked so beautiful and attractive that she could not bear the thought of it being left empty.

She knew that as soon as she had gone the holland covers would be put over the furniture, the flowers thrown out, and the windows shuttered and barred.

Only the garden would come into full bloom with nobody to appreciate it or enjoy its beauty.

She did not walk into the Salon in which she had sat with her father last night, because for the moment to remember the things they had said to each other then was upsetting, but into the Library.

She had only just reached it when Mr. Dutton, her father's secretary, who he had said would manage the house when they had left, followed her.

"Good morning, My Lady," he said. "I was wondering at what time you wish the carriage brought round. Your father has given me a letter to Her Ladyship to explain your unexpected arrival."

Imeldra hesitated for a moment.

"Shall I think about it after I have had breakfast, Mr. Dutton? As I am sure you are aware, I have no wish to arrive before I have to."

She had known Mr. Dutton since she was a child, and now his kind, middle-aged face was filled with sympathy and an expression which told her he knew how she was feeling.

"There's no hurry, My Lady," he said. "And while you're here I suggest you have a look round and see if there is anything you wish to take with you."

"Thank you, Mr. Dutton."

He left her as if he sensed that she wished to be alone, and after spending a little time in the Library she walked to the Breakfast Room where the old Butler who had been at Kingsclere with her mother was waiting to serve her.

He bowed respectfully and since her father was not present arranged the newspapers, which had just arrived, on a silver stand in front of her plate so that she could read while she was eating.

Because she thought it would please him she

glanced at *The Morning Post* while playing with the food she had chosen from half-a-dozen silver *entrée* dishes engraved with the family crest.

Inevitably she remembered how when she and her father were in France they had been quite content with a French breakfast of croissants and coffee.

But in England to have refused the innumerable dishes which had been cooked by the Chef would certainly have upset the household.

As her father had always said laughingly:

"When in Rome we must do as the Romans do."

The Butler moved discreetly from the room and Imeldra, feeling as if food would choke her, pushed aside her plate and picked up the newspaper.

The headlines, as she had expected, told her that there had been innumerable speeches in Parliament for and against the Reform Bill.

Then she looked further down the page.

An item caught her eye and she read it with interest.

The Marquis of Marizon has engaged William Gladwin to rebuild the Orangery at Marizon, his country seat, which was recently destroyed by fire.

Mr. Gladwin, who is an expert on Orangeries, is, it is understood, following the famous Regency architect, Mr. Humphrey Repton, who was the first to include top-lighting in Conservatories and glasshouses. He has also in many mansions incorporated the Orangery, or the winter garden, with the house rather than make it a separate building.

Imeldra read the report twice.

She knew William Gladwin because for three years he had worked at Kingsclere to add the Orangery that for some unknown reason had never been erected before, to the house that had existed since the sixteenth century.

When Gladwin had finished it was a very impressive sight and, in Imeldra's opinion, very beautiful.

She had read later of how Humphrey Repton had come to believe that light was important for plants and had introduced top-lighting, instead of providing light only through the sides of the buildings.

"I wish we had had that here, Papa," Imeldra had said to her father.

"I am quite content with the building as it is," he replied, "and whatever people may say, not only our orange trees but also the orchids and azaleas and all those other unusual plants we brought from Africa are flourishing extremely well."

"Yes, they are," Imeldra agreed, "so why should we be envious of anybody?"

"I never am," the Earl had replied, and she knew it was the truth.

"William Gladwin!" she said to herself now. "He was such a kind man."

She remembered the hours she used to sit watching him work, supervising the bricklayers, then the carpenters and the glaziers, checking everything they did with his plans.

It suddenly struck her that the Marquis of Marizon lived not far away.

She had never met him because her father had once

25

said that he was a very serious young man who did not approve either of him or, as he described it, of the 'goings on of the King.'

Imeldra had been too young at the time to understand what her father had meant by that.

She was quite certain however, that the Marquis must be a bore if he did not approve of her father, and therefore dismissed him from her mind.

Now she thought perhaps she had missed something not as regards the Marquis, but in not seeing Marizon.

She was well aware that it was reputed to be one of the finest houses in the country, and often there were references in the newspapers and magazines to the pictures in the Gallery at Marizon, the furniture and the silver.

'I ought to have persuaded Papa to invite the Marquis here,' she thought.

She then remembered with a little pang of her heart that when her father married Lady Bullington, she would be the hostess at Kingsclere and not herself.

It was then for the first time that it swept over her what it would mean to have her father married and a woman in the place of her mother, and the realisation made her angry.

"How dare any woman aspire to being Papa's wife?" she asked herself, and knew that a great number of women had done just that but failed in their aspirations, while Lady Bullington had succeeded.

The anger that seemed to invade her whole body made her feel suddenly defiant and rebellious.

Because she loved her father so deeply she had

agreed to everything he had said last night, in fact agreeing with him without making any protest.

Now she thought it was intolerable, first that he should leave her, secondly that she should have to go to her grandmother's and thirdly that in the future, her place in her father's life would be taken over by his wife who would by right have priority in everything that concerned her home.

"I cannot bear it!" she said aloud.

Then as she looked down at the newspaper that lay on the table a daring plan came into her mind.

It took her a minute or two to think it out, and when she had done so, there was a light in her eyes which her father would have recognised and understood.

She lifted her chin in a way which, although she did not realise it, was a clear imitation of him.

"I will do it!" she said to herself. "It will be quite easy because there is nobody to stop me!"

chapter two

DRIVING along the country lanes Imeldra enjoyed the beauty of the hedges bursting into bud, the primroses beneath them, and the golden cowslip in the fields.

It was very evident where her father's extensive estate came to an end and that belonging to the Marquis of Marizon began.

Her mother had chosen the deep-sea blue paint which decorated the doors and windows of the thatched cottages which belonged to her father, while those belonging to the Marquis were all painted a dark, rather dull olive green.

At the same time the cottage gardens were bright with spring flowers, the Alms-Houses appeared quite attractive, and the villagers she noticed moving about in the small hamlets were well dressed and there were no ragged children and few tramps.

She had been so seldom in England, apart from her last year at School, that she was able to appraise everything with the inquisitive eye of a foreigner.

She could see that the Marquis's estate was in excellent order and the woods were well suited for both hunting and shooting.

She knew that Baker, the old coachman whom she had known for many years, was surprised when after they had left home and driven for some miles in the direction of her grandmother's house she had knocked on the glass which separated her from the driving-seat.

When the footman climbed down to see what she required she simply said:

"Tell Baker to take me to Marizon."

"Marizon, M'Lady?" the man exclaimed in surprise.

"Marizon," Imeldra insisted and added:

"I am calling on Mr. Gladwin who you will remember once worked at Kingsclere. So please take me to the side-door and do not mention my name to anyone."

She knew that the footman was astonished, but she thought that Baker would doubtless understand.

Anyway, what the servants thought did not particularly concern her, and if she stayed with Mr. Gladwin as she hoped to do, she would send back a note to Mr. Dutton to explain her change of plans.

She had with her the letter which her father had written to her grandmother so that at least nobody would be expecting her, and it was not for Mr. Dutton to criticise what she did, however strange it might appear.

"Anything is better than having to stay for a long time with Grandmama, who will only complain hour after hour, day after day," she told herself.

She had grown very fond of Mr. Gladwin when he was working at Kingsclere.

He was in fact a very unusual and intelligent man.

The son of a yeoman farmer in the North of England, he had been sent to a good School, then to University.

His father intended him either to follow in his footsteps, or else join his uncle who was a well-known solicitor in the part of Yorkshire where they lived.

William Gladwin however had determined that his interest lay in design, and when he left University he apprenticed himself to a distinguished architect and learnt from him everything the man could teach him.

Because he had a great appreciation of flowers he soon specialised in Orangeries, and the Earl, who always liked the best, heard of his success and sent for him to come to Kingsclere.

By this time he was no longer a young man and his reputation had spread the length and breadth of the country.

The Prince Regent, who had talked of employing him, found that the Earl had got there first, and during the three years it took to build the Orangery at Kingsclere Imeldra saw him intermittently and they became friends.

She thought now that it would be a delight to see him again, and she was quite certain she could persuade him to let her stay at Marizon as his assistant, or in some similar capacity, until her aunt came South and she could join her in London.

It was the sort of plan, she thought, that was so like her father's way of thinking that it would amuse him.

At the same time, she hoped he did not hear of it until after he had left England.

The horses turned down a long drive which was bordered by huge lime trees and she had her first sight of Marizon. While she had expected it to be impressive, she had not been prepared for the beauty of it.

It was very different in every way from Kingsclere, and more imposing.

At the moment illuminated by the pale April sunshine, it had a magical appearance with its pale grey stone silhouetted against a background of dark fir trees, its long windows glittered like diamonds.

'It is lovely!' Imeldra thought and was sorry that she could not discuss it and its owner with her father.

The old Marquis had been Lord Lieutenant of the County, but he had been a difficult, somewhat disagreeable old man.

He had been friendly with her father and mother, but after her mother's death he showed his disapproval of her father's raffish behaviour.

He had struck him off his visiting-list, refusing to accept him as Deputy Lieutenant, and to all intents and purposes cut off all communication between the two estates.

Because Imeldra had been so young when all this happened she had never seen Marizon although it was so near to Kingsclere.

Now she thought she had missed a great deal and she made up her mind she would see the pictures and the other treasures the house contained.

This made her all the more determined that William Gladwin should agree to her plan and invite her to be his assistant.

The carriage passed over a bridge which spanned the lake and drove not towards the front door with its great flight of grey stone steps, but round the side of the house.

Here there was a secondary entrance used, Imeldra suspected, not by the servants but by those of the household who occupied the middle status.

"Governesses, secretaries, teachers of all kinds," her mother had once said, "are betwixt Heaven and Hell, and the poor things often, I suspect have a very difficult and lonely time of it in a house like ours."

Imeldra, remembering this, had always been particularly charming to the rather nervous young men who helped Mr. Dutton, and her mother had always been kind to the Governesses and teachers who came to the School Room.

'Now I shall be one of them,' Imeldra thought as she heard her footman asking for Mr. Gladwin.

The maid servant who had opened the door fetched a footman and Imeldra stepped out of the carriage, knowing that Baker would wait and carry out her instructions not to say who she was.

The footman took her through what she knew were the back corridors of the house, then through a magnificent Hall, where she had no time to look around, and along more corridors hung with pictures.

The footman was obviously in a hurry and moved more quickly than if she had come to the front door.

Finally when they reached what she was aware was the other side of the house he indicated with his hand a great mass of stone and bricks on which a number of workmen were occupied.

"You'll find Mr. Gladwin here, Miss," he said abruptly.

He walked away, while Imeldra stepped out through the door over the floor of a building that was being added to the house.

The walls of the new Orangery were so far only about four feet high, but she could already see how impressive the design would be. There would be many more windows than was usual, besides, as she suspected, the innovation of a glass roof.

For the moment, however, she was not concerned with the building, but with the man who had designed it, and she saw his grey head about the piles of bricks as he gave orders to the workmen.

She hurried towards him unaware that in her pretty spring travelling-gown covered with a light silk pelisse and wearing a bonnet trimmed with ribbons the colour of the sky, she looked like one of the flowers which would later bloom in the Orangery.

She had reached Mr. Gladwin's side before he turned and saw her.

For a moment he stared as if he could hardly believe his eyes. Then as Imeldra's hands went out towards him he exclaimed:

"Lady Imeldra! What are you doing here?"

Imeldra laughed.

"I was half-afraid you had forgotten me."

"As if I could do that," William Gladwin replied. "But I had no idea you were in England. Is your father with you?"

He looked over her shoulder as if expecting to see the Earl coming from the house.

"I want to talk to you privately," Imeldra said.

"Yes, of course," Mr. Gladwin agreed with a puzzled expression in his eyes.

He led the way to where erected on the lawn was a small wooden hut, with a front door and several windows.

As it was the same sort of hut he had used at Kingsclere, Imeldra was not surprised to find that it contained not only a large table on which were strewn his designs, and several serviceable chairs but also a comfortable one beside a stove which gave out good heat in the winter months.

"It is just the same as you had at Kingsclere!" she exclaimed. "You always manage to make yourself comfortable!"

"As I told you then," Mr. Gladwin smiled, "a man works better when he's warm, well fed, and of course well housed."

Imeldra laughed.

"I remember that."

Mr. Gladwin shut the door and Imeldra sat down in the comfortable chair while he drew up another beside her.

"Now, what do you want to tell me?" he asked and added quickly before she could reply: "There's nothing wrong with the Orangery at Kingsclere?"

"No, no it is perfect!" Imeldra said. "And the flowers are flourishing."

Actually she had not had time to see it yesterday after her arrival, but she knew how it would upset him if he thought anything had gone wrong with what he considered one of 'his children.'

"I am here," she went on, "because I want to stay with you for a little while."

"Stay with me?" William Gladwin exclaimed.

"Yes, Mr. Gladwin. Papa has to go abroad and he has told me I must go to stay with my grandmother, which I have no wish to do. So please, let me come to you. It may only be for a few days until my aunt, the Duchess of Ilminister, returns to London."

She saw that Mr. Gladwin was too astonished for the moment to reply and she went on:

"I suspect you are well aware of the feelings that existed between the late Marquis and Papa, so of course I could not stay with you under my own name. But if you think I would be useless as an assistant, you might allow me to be your granddaughter."

Imeldra had only just thought of this, and looking at Mr. Gladwin she thought that if her grandfathers were alive she would have liked them to look like him.

William Gladwin when he was young had been quite a handsome man, and in his old age he now looked really distinguished.

He had a broad, intelligent forehead beneath a quite surprisingly profuse amount of silver hair.

His features were clear-cut, and Imeldra suspected that somewhere in his family there was Viking blood from the invaders who had come across the North Sea to carry off the cattle, ravage the women and sail away in their strange looking craft.

Whatever the source of his good looks, William Gladwin was a man anyone would be proud to acknowledge as a relative.

She said now with a little smile:

"Please let me be your granddaughter. I would love you really to be my grandfather."

After a moment of incredulous astonishment Mr. Gladwin threw back his head and laughed.

"Only you, Lady Imeldra, could think of anything so outrageous," he exclaimed, "but much as I would love to have you with me, you must know it is impossible."

Imeldra settled herself a little more comfortably in the chair and started to argue, confident as she talked that she was being very convincing.

She was not prepared to go into the details of why her father had most reluctantly to leave her, but she had the idea that William Gladwin, who was a very perceptive man, would guess why.

She went on to explain how she had run away from School and had no intention of going back; that she dreaded having to stay with her grandmother; and how much she resented being pitchforked against her will into Society as a débutante and having to live with her aunt until she married.

She had no idea as she talked how revealing her story was, but as Mr. Gladwin listened attentively Imeldra was sure she was winning her case.

"If you will not have me," she finally announced, "I have a good mind to go off somewhere on my own and I am sure Papa would not approve of that!"

"You are blackmailing me!" Mr. Gladwin exclaimed. "To do that might get you into a great deal of trouble."

He thought as he spoke that it was quite impossible for him to allow this lovely young woman, who had grown spectacularly beautiful since he had last seen her, to be on her own.

He shuddered at the thought of her becoming involved with strange men, and he was quite certain that looking as she did she would be the prey not only of fortune-hunters but of thieves.

He gave a sigh. Then he said:

"You make it very difficult for me to re—"

"You will let me stay? You will really let me stay?" Imeldra interrupted. "It will be such fun! We will be able to talk in the way we used to do at Kingsclere when Papa was busy with his friends and my Governess was bored with me for asking her too many questions which she could not answer."

Mr. Gladwin smiled.

"You were certainly a very inquisitive little girl."

"And now I am an inquisitive young woman," Imeldra added, "and only you can give me the answers I want to hear."

"Very well," Mr. Gladwin said. "I agree to what you suggest, but under protest! I suppose you have brought your luggage with you?"

"Not as much as you might fear," Imeldra replied, "only the clothes I had at School. Later I shall need wardrobes of new gowns with which to dazzle London!"

The way she spoke made it sound less glamorous than her words, and Mr. Gladwin knew that in fact she was rather apprehensive of what her life would be like.

He was also well aware how much Imeldra would miss her father.

All through his long life he had never known a father and daughter who not only were so fond of each other, but who were both such outstanding characters in their own ways.

He not only liked the Earl but admired him, and understood as few other people did that his dashing reputation was inevitable since he was such a handsome man with a magnetic quality about him that made him irresistable to women.

He thought now that Imeldra, who had been the most entrancing, intelligent and delightful little girl he had ever known, would prove irresistible to men and he could only pray that she would find the right sort of husband to love and protect her.

At the same time, going from great house to great house, William Gladwin had an inside knowledge of Society which few people who did not belong to it were in a position to have.

It made him cynical about the dashing young aristocrats who left their great ancestral homes in the country for months so that they could gamble in the Clubs and gaming halls in London, throwing away money which could be better spent on building houses for their pensioners or improving their farms.

'She is too good for one of that sort,' William Gladwin thought to himself as he looked at Imeldra.

Aloud he said:

"His Lordship's away from home at the moment, and therefore if I tell the Housekeeper that my granddaughter has come to stay with me, I do not think she'll be particularly interested one way or the other."

"That is good," Imeldra said. "Thank you, thank you dear Mr. Gladwin—or rather 'Grandpapa' as I shall call you now—for having me. It has made me very happy."

"That is what I have always wanted you to be," Mr. Gladwin said in a low voice. "I often thought you were at times, a very sad little girl without your mother."

The way he spoke unexpectedly brought the tears to Imeldra's eyes, and she replied:

"Only you could understand that, although I adore Papa and have always been happy with him, I can never forget Mama and sometimes I feel she is near me."

"I am sure she is," Mr. Gladwin said quietly.

As he spoke he rose to open the door and say in a more practical tone:

"I'll go and find the Housekeeper, and I expect you'll want to tell your coachman that you are staying."

"Yes, of course," Imeldra answered, "but I doubt if I can find my way back to the door through which I came in."

Mr. Gladwin raised his eyebrows as she explained:

"I thought it was correct to use the side-door and also I had no wish to encounter the Marquis before you had agreed to have me."

"That was sensible," Mr. Gladwin approved. "At the same time, as I have already said, His Lordship's away from home."

"Has he a wife?" Imeldra asked as they stepped out of the hut into the mess of bricks and stonework.

Mr. Gladwin did not answer, which she thought a little strange until she understood that it would be a mistake to talk intimately while there were workmen about.

Imeldra then sent her carriage home with a note she hastily scribbled to Mr. Dutton saying that a friend of hers was staying at Marizon, and she was going to stay there with her for two or three days before continuing her journey to her grandmother.

She made no explanations, feeling that what she did was not any business of Mr. Dutton's. But just in case he should try to communicate with her at her grandmother's she thought it wise to let him know where she actually was.

She gave the note to Baker herself, telling him to leave as soon as her luggage had been carried into the house and once again impressing on him in a low voice not to let anybody at Marizon know her real name.

She knew the old coachman was somewhat bewildered by her insistence, but that at the same time he would obey her.

He was too good a servant and also too used to her father to query any orders he was given.

As the luggage was carried into the house Imeldra felt with a little feeling of excitement that this was an adventure.

It had, in fact, been a desperate action to avoid staying with her grandmother, but now that she was actually in Marizon and realised how much there was to see in the great house she felt she was starting a journey into the unknown!

Mr. Gladwin had been allotted a quite pleasant bedroom and a Sitting-Room in the East Wing, and the Housekeeper arranged that Imeldra should have the bedroom next to it.

It was a pretty room, and yet Imeldra was aware that it would not compare in any way with the grandeur she expected to find in the State Bedrooms.

But it was comfortable, the windows overlooked

the lake at the front of the house and one of the housemaids was told to unpack for her.

She was a bright, cheerful looking country girl who Imeldra guessed had not long come to work at the big house and was thrilled to be allotted a young lady to look after on her own.

"Oi 'opes as Oi pleases you, Miss."

"I am sure you will," Imeldra answered, and told her exactly how she liked her clothes arranged.

Because her father had always given her a generous allowance her clothes at School were extremely expensive and very beautifully made.

She had been the envy and admiration of all the other girls of her age.

Her travels in her father's company had developed not only her intelligence but also her good taste.

Imeldra knew both what were the correct clothes to wear, and also that they should be a frame for the person who wore them and be compatible with her personality.

Now she thought it was a good thing that her gowns were fairly simple and therefore not too elaborate or showy for the part she was to play as William Gladwin's granddaughter.

She changed from the gown in which she had travelled into one of white silk, with large sleeves and a full skirt which accentuated her tiny waist.

When she went downstairs to find her supposed grandfather she was aware that when she passed through the Hall the footmen looked at her in admiration.

One of them even gave her a cheeky smile which he would not have done had he been aware of her real rank.

She found that William Gladwin was still busy with his workmen and after listening to him giving instructions for a little while she went back into the house.

She moved slowly down the corridors stopping to look at every picture, then at the furniture, knowing everything was a delight.

It was not surprising, she thought, that Marizon had always been spoken of almost with bated breath by her father's friends in the past.

She enjoyed herself so much that she was quite surprised when William Gladwin joined her to say that the work for the day was done and he was now free to go to his Sitting-Room.

After enjoying a good tea, Imeldra settled down on a comfortable sofa saying, as she did so:

"Now tell me everything you have been doing since we last met."

William Gladwin told her of how he had made some improvements to the Orangery at Hanbury Hall at Droitwich, and then as if this was her real interest for the moment Imeldra said:

"Now tell me what you think about this house, and of course its owner."

"Have you ever met the Marquis?" Mr. Gladwin asked.

Imeldra shook her head.

"I think it would be a mistake for you to do so."

"Why do you say that?" she enquired. "Tell me the truth, Mr. Gladwin. Has he a raffish reputation like Papa? As you must be aware, that would not shock me."

Mr. Gladwin smiled as if at her frankness. Then he said:

"The Marquis is a very unusual man, and certainly

different from what I expected when he asked me to design his Orangery."

"In what way?"

"He's extremely intelligent, and I suppose from a lady's point of view, very attractive."

"Then what is wrong with him?"

"There's nothing wrong, Lady Imeldra," Mr. Gladwin said quickly. "It's just that there's something which I do not understand."

Imeldra was wide eyed with curiosity.

"What do you mean by that?"

"I don't exactly know," Mr. Gladwin answered. "But I suppose from years of working in houses like this I have come to sense the atmosphere, so to speak."

"And what's the atmosphere at Marizon?"

"I wish I could put it into words, not only to you, but to myself."

"Then what do you feel?"

"I feel there's something wrong—something unnatural."

Imeldra looked alight with interest as she asked:

"Do you mean ghosts? Or is the Marquis being threatened by Highwaymen? Perhaps a wicked Heir Presumptive, as he is not married?"

"I doubt if it's any of those things," Mr. Gladwin answered, "and I cannot understand why I'm telling you this at all, except perhaps it is a relief to talk to somebody about it."

"I want you to talk to me," Imeldra said. "Tell me exactly what you feel."

"I wish I knew," William Gladwin said unhappily. "There is a reserve about the Marquis, although there is no reason why he should not be reserved with me.

44

I have the feeling that when I am with him he's not exactly afraid of something, but at the same time on guard, if not slightly apprehensive. No! Words are inadequate. I can't explain what it is."

"I find what you are telling me fascinating," Imeldra answered. "I do wish Papa was with us. He would love a puzzle of this sort."

As she spoke she thought perhaps her father would not be so interested in the problems and difficulties of a man as he would be in those of a woman, and this puzzle was something she must solve for herself.

An intrigue was the last thing she had expected.

She knew William Gladwin well enough to know that he would not have spoken of it if it had not in fact been troubling him, and it was therefore a definite problem.

He talked and Imeldra learned a little more about the Marquis, until it was time to change for dinner.

Her maid, whose name she discovered was Emma, brought her a bath and she put on another pretty, but simple gown.

Then she and William Gladwin dined, not in his Sitting-Room but in another room also in the East Wing which was furnished as a small Dining-Room.

They were waited on by two footmen and the food, Imeldra was glad to find, was delicious.

There was also a claret which Mr. Gladwin enjoyed, although Imeldra preferred lemonade.

When finally they both retired to bed Imeldra felt she had spent a delightful evening and tomorrow she would start to explore the house.

Perhaps in her explorings she would find an answer to what was upsetting the Marquis to the point where his discomfort was obvious to the man who was building his Orangery.

* * *

The morning dawned full of sunshine and it was warm enough for Imeldra to walk in the garden without a shawl.

She entered it correctly by way of the Orangery, then moved away across the lawns past the flower-beds, appreciating as she compared it with Kingsclere how charmingly this garden was laid out and how well the gardeners had done their work.

"The Marquis is obviously very particular," she told herself, "and like Papa aims for perfection."

It was another point on the credit side of his character which Imeldra felt she must assess in detail before she could begin to discover what Mr. Gladwin knew instinctively was wrong.

Last night after dinner she had said to him:

"I am very intrigued with what you have told me about the Marquis."

"I think perhaps it is something I should not have said," Mr. Gladwin replied ruefully, "but I console myself by thinking you will not be here for long, so it is doubtful if you will ever meet His Lordship."

"Can you imagine how frustrating it will be to leave here wondering what is still undiscovered and puzzling about his manner for the rest of my life?"

William Gladwin laughed.

"That is the last thing you will do! Once you are in London with Her Grace you will be a huge success. They will toast you in the Clubs and you will receive many compliments. There will be other Gentlemen for you to think about, instead of Marizon and its Marquis."

The way he spoke told Imeldra better than words that he was deeply regretting having been confidential in the first place.

Because she thought it would be a mistake for him to worry about her she replied casually:

"I am sure you are right, and once I leave here and cease to be your granddaughter I suppose the barriers between our estates will be up again and I shall be on one side of them and His Lordship the other."

She saw an expression of relief in Mr. Gladwin's eyes, which made her more keen than ever to find out what had upset him in the first place, or rather what was wrong with the Marquis.

The green lawns ended in a Water Garden out of which led a Herb Garden, and beyond that a shrubbery which Imeldra was aware would be very beautiful once the rhododendrons came into bloom.

By the time she had finished exploring the garden it was time for luncheon, and because Mr. Gladwin could not spare much time from his work, this was brought to the little wooden hut.

Imeldra enjoyed picnicking there although it was a very light meal. As soon as William Gladwin had hurried back to see what his workmen were doing, she decided she would now have a more thorough look inside the house.

The sunshine of the morning was now overcast with clouds and it was not as warm as it had been before.

She therefore thought it was a practical idea to

inspect the State Rooms and in particular the Picture Gallery of which she had heard so much.

It was rather exciting to think that because its owner was away she could have the huge house all to herself apart from the servants.

She thought they were very likely relaxing when their master was not in residence, and she was sure of this when she noticed there was only one footman on duty in the Hall, and he was reading a newspaper.

She went into the Library to find, as she had anticipated, that it was magnificent.

She remembered reading somewhere that the Marizon Library included a first folio of Shakespeare's plays and a copy of the Gutenberg Bible.

There was a catalogue lying on one of the tables, but for the moment she wished to see the pictures rather than linger among the books.

So telling herself that the Library was a place to which she would return, she went from there into the Salon.

This was a large, very impressive room hung with huge crystal chandeliers, and the walls were covered, which she had not expected, with white green-veined marble which was very lovely.

There was some magnificent pictures by Reynolds which were in keeping with its grandeur, and Imeldra looked at them for a long time before she left the Salon to walk towards where she guessed the Picture Gallery would be.

She was not wrong and found the long gallery running half the length of the centre part of the house, filled with pictures that at first glance made her gasp.

There were Van Dycks, Rembrandts, Rubenses,

Poussins, haphazardly hung it seemed to her surprise, according to no particular scheme of arrangement, although each one in its own way was so superb that it was difficult when she was looking at it to think of anything but that particular picture.

Then half-way down the long wall, which faced the high windows framed in embroidered brocade each with a draped pelmet surmounted with gold carvings, she stopped in front of a picture which for a moment puzzled her.

Then as she was staring at it she heard footsteps behind her and knew that William Gladwin had joined her.

She had told him where she would be and hoped that he would find time to leave his workmen so that they could enjoy the treasures of the house together.

"I am glad you have come," she said without turning round. "Can you imagine that anybody with any artistic perception could allow this obvious fake to be hung here amongst all these masterpieces? The Marquis must be a fool, or blind!"

The footsteps had stopped behind her and a voice which she did not know remarked dryly:

"I can assure you that I am neither of those things!"

Imeldra turned round sharply.

Standing a few feet from her was not William Gladwin, as she had supposed, but a tall, broad-shouldered man.

He was exquisitely dressed, his white cravat intricately tied, his champagne-coloured pantaloons ending in Hessian boots so polished that they reflected his surroundings.

For the moment she was not concerned with his

clothes but with his face, and she thought that while he was distinguished and good-looking, though not handsome in the same way that her father was, he had an unmistakable expression of cynicism and bitterness that was quite remarkable.

What was more his eyes were hard, and he was staring at her in a manner that was penetrating and at the same time almost insulting.

For a moment they just looked at each other. Then the newcomer said:

"Who are you? And what are you doing in my Gallery without my permission?"

Quite unabashed Imeldra dropped him a respectful curtsy before she replied:

"Forgive me if I am intruding, but I understood that Your Lordship was not in residence."

"I have returned unexpectedly, but I see no reason why that should entitle you not only to be here, but to criticise my pictures."

There was a faint smile on Imeldra's lips as she said:

"Now I have seen Your Lordship I am sure that you are as well aware as I am that I was not being impertinent or ignorant in referring to the picture behind me as being a fake that should not have been hung here."

"We are not discussing my pictures," the Marquis answered coldly, "but you, and you have not replied to my question."

"As to my identity? I came here unexpectedly to visit my grandfather, William Gladwin. He was certain that Your Lordship would not refuse to let me stay with him for a night or two."

"You are William Gladwin's granddaughter?" the Marquis asked.

He spoke in a way which told Imeldra he could hardly believe it to be true, and she replied quickly:

"My name is Imeldra Gladwin, and may I, now that you are here, Your Lordship, thank you for your hospitality, and hope that I do not intrude."

"No, of course not," the Marquis said as if there was nothing else he could say. "At the same time, Miss Gladwin, I hope you will retract your assertion that I am a fool."

"I thought I had already done so, My Lord."

There was a faint twitch to the Marquis's lips as he said:

"You speak as if you are knowledgeable about pictures, which is surprising seeing how young you appear to be."

"Knowledge does not always come with age, My Lord, but with intuition, which cannot be taught, but can only be inborn."

Again there was the suspicion of a smile on the Marquis's lips before he said:

"If you have that sort of intuition, Miss Gladwin, I suggest you use it to find a reason why I have not rearranged the pictures in this Gallery and removed what you so rightly called a fake."

Imeldra put her head a little to one side as she tried to find the answer to her question.

Because she was looking directly at him she felt as if she could read his thoughts.

"I think, My Lord," she said, "the answer you wish me to give is that you have not yet had the time to arrange the Picture Gallery but..."

She paused before she continued slowly:

"But I think it is more than that . . . something . . . I cannot quite understand . . . tells me you are . . . reluctant . . . to do so."

There was a look of incredulity in the Marquis's eyes before he asked harshly:

"Why should you say that? What are you insinuating?"

He spoke in a manner which told Imeldra he was upset.

"I am sorry . . ." she said quickly. "But you did . . . ask me!"

Then, as if he thought he had over-reacted, he said in a very different tone of voice:

"There have been so many other things to move around in the house, and the Picture Gallery has been left until the last."

He looked to his right and left as he spoke, and almost as if he was acting in fact, he added:

"There is a great deal to do."

"That I understand," Imeldra said, "and I thought the Salon which is next to the Library is magnificent and exactly as it should be."

"I am, of course, glad that it meets with your approval, Miss Gladwin," the Marquis said, and now he was undoubtedly being sarcastic.

Imeldra gave a little laugh.

"Why are you laughing?" he asked sharply.

"Because it obviously irritates you that I should presume either to praise or to criticise just because I am young. If I were supported on two crutches you would doubtless listen to me with respect, whether my opinions deserved it or not."

She paused before she continued:

"Only the English are so obsessed with age. Foreigners are much more inclined to appreciate one's intelligence and not count the years."

Now the Marquis looked definitely amused.

"You talk as if you have travelled a great deal."

"Actually I have," Imeldra said, "but again I cannot think, except that you are English, why it should surprise you."

"You are making my nationality sound a disadvantage," the Marquis parried, "although I have always thought it something of which I should be both proud and grateful."

"That is the average Englishman's attitude," Imeldra answered. "He is also supremely sure that everything he thinks is right, and that once he crosses the Channel he is consorting with illiterates and barbarians, not to add a few cannibals here and there!"

She spoke teasingly as she might have spoken to her father, and she knew that the Marquis was looking at her in such surprise that for the moment it swept away the cynical boredom which she was certain was his habitual expression.

Because she thought she had given him enough to think about she merely said:

"May I, with Your Lordship's permission, continue to view your Gallery, or would you rather I returned to my grandfather?"

"I certainly think you should tell me more about my pictures and indeed myself," the Marquis said. "I find you, Miss Gladwin, a very surprising young woman."

"I am glad about that."

"Why?"

"Because surprises are always interesting. When people are exactly what one expects them to be like, I find that a definite bore."

"I suppose having said that in a very provocative manner," the Marquis remarked, "you are expecting me to ask you if I am what you expected."

Imeldra hesitated for a moment. Then she said:

"That is certainly a leading question, and as I presume Your Lordship would like an answer, let me tell you the answer is 'yes' and 'no.'"

"Explain!" the Marquis ordered.

"I thought perhaps you would look different from the average Beau or Buck, whichever you consider yourself to be. But there is something else."

"What is it?"

There was a pause before Imeldra said:

"I think Your Lordship must allow me time to consider my answer to that question. I might not be accurate in my considerations and, as I have already said, you are different and perhaps I should add . . . defensively . . . a little difficult."

Unexpectedly the Marquis laughed.

"I just do not believe this conversation is taking place," he said. "I came home expecting to be alone this evening, as I have some papers to work on, and was in fact considerably bored by the idea. If I am 'different,' Miss Gladwin, you are certainly a surprise, and I must ask you to dine with me."

Imeldra hesitated for a moment knowing this was something she would very much like to do and wondering how she could accept.

After a moment she said demurely:

"I think Your Lordship has forgotten that I have come here to be with my grandfather."

"I feel sure Gladwin will understand," the Marquis said casually.

"I shall of course have to ask his permission."

"Are you making difficulties?"

"I am behaving, as Your Lordship is well aware, with propriety."

"That is invariably, as I have found, very boring."

Imeldra raised her eyebrows.

"That is not what I have heard about you."

"What have you heard?" he asked challengingly.

"That you are serious-minded and censorious of those who speak out of turn or behave unconventionally."

She was thinking of her father as she spoke and how unkind and disagreeable the Marquis's father had been to him.

She had no idea that her voice had sharpened and there was almost a bitter note in the way she spoke.

After a moment he asked:

"What have I done to make you speak like that?"

Imeldra felt she had been indiscreet.

"The things one hears about people are often incorrect. At the same time, as my Nanny used to say: 'There's no smoke without a fire!'"

"That is an infuriating reply," the Marquis retorted.

"I think, My Lord," Imeldra said quickly, "that on such short acquaintance I have already been far too personal to be correct."

"What is this insistence where I am concerned that

you should be so proper and correct?" the Marquis asked. "If that is indeed my reputation, which I very much doubt, it is not of my choosing."

Imeldra did not reply. She merely looked at him mockingly and after a moment he said:

"I sent for my Agent, and he will be waiting for me. Will you promise to dine with me? Meet me in the Salon at seven-thirty."

Imeldra hesitated and he added:

"If you prefer, I will speak to your grandfather myself."

There was a note in his voice that told Imeldra that he would make it an order, and she was certain he would upset William Gladwin, which was something she did not want.

"I will tell him," she said, "and if he forbids me to dine with you, you will understand that I would not wish to disobey anyone of whom I am so fond."

"I shall understand nothing of the sort!" the Marquis replied. "I wish to continue this conversation, and as a guest you must not only accede to your host's wishes, but also appreciate that he has his rights."

Imeldra laughed and her laughter seemed to ring out round the whole Gallery.

"How could I refuse an invitation which is a mixture of a request, a challenge, and of course blackmail?"

She dropped the Marquis a curtsy.

"I shall look forward, My Lord, to our dinner together."

The Marquis stared at her again as if he could not believe she was real.

Then he walked away, his foot-steps ringing out

on the polished parquet floor and continuing down the passage beyond the Gallery until there was only silence.

Imeldra stood where he had left her watching until he was out of sight.

Then she thought with a feeling of delight that this was far more exciting, far more intriguing than if she was with her grandmother.

Almost as if she felt it her duty she continued to look at the pictures, but she knew she was now not thinking about them.

Instead she was aware of exactly what William Gladwin had mentioned when he had told her that there was something about the Marquis that was different, or indeed wrong.

Why was he so cynical when he had everything in life—looks, wealth, possessions, rank, and one of the finest houses in England? And doubtless a large number of relatives who thought that everything he did was marvellous.

Imeldra's intuition told her that what she felt vibrating from him was in no way springing from happiness, contentment or even pride of possession.

There was something wrong, very, very wrong, and she was determined to find out what it was!

chapter three

WHEN she reached the end of the Picture Gallery, Imeldra went to find William Gladwin.

She had been expecting him to come, but when she arrived at the building site he was just locking up the wooden hut for the night.

As she reached him he said:

"I'm sorry, I was delayed and therefore unable to join you as I promised.

"I had somebody else to talk to instead," Imeldra said.

William Gladwin looked at her sharply.

"The Marquis has returned and he has asked me to dine with him tonight."

There was a frown between Mr. Gladwin's eyes.

"I didn't mean this to happen," he said. "I don't know what your father would say."

"I am quite sure that Papa would not object to my dining with the Marquis, although he would think it insulting that you were not included in the invitation."

William Gladwin laughed.

"I assure you, Lady Imeldra, I do not aspire to such heights. My patrons are very kind to me, but I don't eat with them in their Dining-Rooms."

"Then I suppose," Imeldra replied, "if I were really your granddaughter I should refuse our host and make it clear that either you accompany me, or I dine up-stairs."

William Gladwin hesitated before he replied. Then as if he found a solution he said:

"I have the answer to that. Come with me!"

He walked towards the house, and because she felt he wanted to do things his own way, Imeldra did not question him as they walked down the long passage which led to the Hall.

Now that the Marquis had returned there were four footmen and the Butler on duty. William Gladwin walked up to the latter and said:

"Would you be kind enough to give a message to His Lordship?"

"Of course, Mr. Gladwin."

"Will you say that I thank him for his kind invitation to dine with him this evening, but I'm sure he'll understand that I'm very tired after a long day's work. However my granddaughter, Miss Imeldra, will be honoured to be his guest."

Without waiting for the Butler's reply William Gladwin started to climb the magnificent carved stair-case and Imeldra hurriedly followed him.

When they were out of earshot of the servants she said with a little chuckle:

"That was very clever of you."

"I'm not certain if I have done the right thing," Mr. Gladwin said in a low voice, "but at least the staff will not gossip about your being singled out by His Lordship. As you well know, it is an invitation he would not have made to you, if he knew who you are."

"That makes it all the more fun!"

"At the same time, I'm worried," William Gladwin said as they walked along the corridor to the East Wing.

"There is no need to be," Imeldra replied. "I can look after myself, and I will find it very amusing to discover how the noble Marquis behaves when he is not in the company of a Lady from the *Beau Monde.*"

She thought her reply made Mr. Gladwin look more worried than ever, and being half-afraid that he would try to prevent her from dining alone with the Marquis, as soon as they reached the East Wing she told him that she was going to rest and went into her bedroom.

Actually she sat thinking about the Marquis, puzzling as to why he looked so cynical and bitter.

She wondered especially why he had spoken harshly when she told him she thought he had some reason for leaving the fake picture in the Gallery.

The more she thought about it, the more strange it seemed.

In every other part of the house she had seen so far—granted it was very little, considering the size of Marizon—everything had seemed so perfect.

The pictures, the furniture, the china were all exactly right and as she had expected them to be.

Then why in the most important room in the house from a connoisseur's point of view had he deliberately left a fake?

It was impossible to find the answer, and yet the problem both intrigued and excited her while she was dressing for dinner.

Because she wanted to make him more puzzled than he was already, she deliberately chose one of the gowns she had ordered from London before she left School, which was more sophisticated than her others.

At the same time, when she entered the Salon where the Marquis was waiting, it was impossible for her to look anything but very young and very spring-like.

The light from the chandeliers brought out the red in her hair, and sparkled in the tiny diamond dew-drops with which her gown was embroidered.

Imeldra walked slowly towards him with the grace that had been the pride of her dancing teacher, despite the fact that it came to her naturally.

As she reached the Marquis she dropped him a small curtsy, and looking up into his eyes as she rose, she was sure there was a glint of admiration in them.

"Good evening, My Lord," she said. "I hope you received my grandfather's message regretting that he was unable to dine with you this evening."

"I received it," the Marquis replied with a twist of his lips.

"I feel guilty at leaving the poor old man by himself," Imeldra said, "but he gets very tired when he works so hard to please you, and I feel it is important for him to rest when he wishes to do so."

"I get the point, Miss Gladwin," the Marquis said dryly, "that you are correcting my manners and attempting to make me feel guilty."

Because she liked his perceptiveness and the manner in which he challenged her, Imeldra laughed, and she thought as she did so that there was an answering twinkle in the Marquis's dark eyes.

"May I offer you a glass of champagne?" he asked.

"Thank you," Imeldra replied, "but only a little."

"That is what I intended to give you," the Marquis said. "You look too young to drink alcohol of any sort."

Imeldra gave a little sigh.

"We are back on the endless controversy of age," she said, "so I am sure, My Lord, you will not be surprised if I retire to bed early."

It was now the Marquis's turn to laugh and he said:

"You are certainly refreshingly frank, Miss Gladwin, and I think it is the first time I have ever dined with a lady who had warned me in the first five minutes that I might bore her."

"I am glad to be original," Imeldra said, taking the glass of champagne from him, "though I should imagine it is quite difficult to be so, seeing that Your Lordship has such a very wide acquaintance."

She had seated herself while he was fetching her the champagne on a sofa covered with satin in a Boucher blue, and she was aware as she did so that it was a very appropriate frame for her white gown and her red-gold hair.

The Marquis sat down beside her, turning a little sideways so that he could look at her, with his arm along the back of the sofa.

"As you have just said, we keep talking of age," he remarked. "But I am indeed curious to know, unless you have sold your soul to the Devil in exchange for a beautiful face, how you have acquired the self-assurance and intelligence of a woman who has lived for at least thirty years in a very sophisticated world."

"Now you are paying me a compliment," Imeldra exclaimed, "something which has been lamentably lacking in our conversation up to now."

"What do you want me to say?" the Marquis asked. "What hundreds of men must have told you already? That you are very lovely?"

His eyes flickered over her, from her hair to her feet in a manner which Imeldra found slightly insulting.

Then she remembered that she had in fact, invited such familiarity, since it was unlikely that any débutante straight out of the School-Room would speak in such a way and certainly would not dine with him alone.

"To him I am not a débutante," she told herself, "but the granddaughter of a man he has employed to work for him."

But because she was quite certain that once she was under her aunt's chaperonage she would never again be able to talk to a man with such frankness, she was determined to make the most of it.

It might be reckless, it might be slightly reprehensible, but if it was, what did it matter?

Her father was behaving in a far more reckless

way, and if in many respects she was her father's daughter, it was hardly her fault.

After what was quite a long pause, having sipped her champagne to give herself time to think, Imeldra said:

"Thank you, My Lord. Now you make me feel that I am not out of place in this very beautiful room surrounded by such a breath-taking collection of treasures that they must make you very proud."

"Do you really need my reassurance to tell you that you shine dazzlingly amongst them?" the Marquis asked.

There was undoubtedly a mocking note in his voice and Imeldra replied:

"No, I am not ashamed to be amongst them. In fact I feel as I always do when I see beauty as if it becomes a part of me, which nothing can take away. I was, in fact, just concerned with your feelings."

She knew again she had surprised him and the Marquis said:

"I want you to explain to me exactly what you mean by saying you feel that any beautiful thing you see becomes part of you."

"It is difficult to put into words," Imeldra said. "But I knew when I was standing in the ruins of the Temple of Apollo at Delphi and looked down at the view which had enthralled Apollo when he leapt ashore and made that part of Greece his own, that in the passing of a second it was as much mine as it was his."

She spoke very softly, thinking back and reliving the magical moment which had been engraved on her mind and heart.

Then she looked at the Marquis and saw that he was staring at her not so much with surprise or astonishment but with a kind of stupefaction.

"Now I know I am dreaming," he said. "You are not real but have stepped out of one of my pictures to confound me, or dropped in from a passing star."

"I will arrive by whichever method you prefer."

She meant to speak lightly, but somehow as she spoke the words sounded sincere and as she glanced at the Marquis it was difficult to look away.

All through dinner they sparred and duelled with each other in words, Imeldra doing everything in her power to surprise and provoke him.

She was aware as the evening wore on that the Marquis's look of cynicism seemed to wear off and his eyes were no longer as hard as they had been when they first met.

She knew too that when he laughed, which was frequently, the old Butler who waited on them seemed surprised, as if it was a sound that was not often heard at Marizon.

The dinner was delicious and the Marquis looked magnificent sitting at the head of the table which was decorated with gold candelabra and ornaments which exceeded both in age and value, those at Kingsclere.

This was slightly irritating to Imeldra but she was also aware that at Kingsclere the atmosphere was a much happier one than that at Marizon, which as William Gladwin had already discovered had something wrong with it.

She kept asking herself what it could possibly be and was aware that the discrepancy, if that was the right word for it, came from the Marquis himself.

As dinner progressed and she both amused and bemused him, she was aware that he relaxed.

But there was still something she could not understand—a reserve, a tension, something within himself which she could feel so strongly that it was almost possible to reach out and touch it.

Imeldra had had a sensitivity or an instinct, whatever one liked to call it, of her own ever since her childhood.

She could remember when she was small her Nanny saying to her:

"You are fey, that's what you are! If you're not careful you'll grow up to be a Witch. Then where will you be?"

"Flying on a broom-stick!" Imeldra had replied.

Her Nanny had not thought it funny.

As she grew older she found she could assess people's characters as soon as she met them and was seldom mistaken.

"I hate that woman!" she had said once to her mother after a guest left. "She is bad!"

Her mother had looked at her in surprise.

"Why do you say that, dearest? I cannot say Lady Bury is somebody I would wish to be my closest friend, but I know nothing about her to her discredit."

"She is bad, and one day you will know that I am right," Imeldra had insisted.

Two years later the lady in question had been accused of cruelty to a stable-lad who she thought was not looking after her horses properly.

She had beaten him so severely with a riding-crop that the boy's parents had taken him to the Magistrates to protest at the injuries he had suffered.

No charge was proved, but so much scandal had reverberated against Lady Bury that she had been forced to go abroad.

At School, Imeldra had been plagued by girls wishing her to read their fortune, and it was something she had found far too easy to be enjoyable.

She had known as soon as she was friends with them exactly what sort of life they would lead.

The majority likely to follow the pattern of any young woman's in the social world; first a marriage arranged by an ambitious mother, thereafter a dull existence producing babies in the country while her aristocratic husband enjoyed himself in London.

Occasionally she sensed tragedy or despair, and quickly avoided telling the girl what was in store for her, except where she thought it was possible to warn her in a subtle manner.

It was a gift of which Imeldra was not proud, and she usually found it more an inconvenience than a pleasure, as she had told her father.

"Your grandmother was Scottish," he had answered. "There is also Irish blood in you, and my father was very proud of his Cornish ancestry."

His eyes twinkled as he finished:

"In other words, my darling, you are a mongrel with an abnormal amount of Celt in your blood. How then can you be anything but clairvoyant?"

"It is a nuisance, Papa," Imeldra complained. "It means I get to know all about anyone I meet far too quickly, and certainly miss a lot of fun."

Her father had laughed again.

"You should be grateful instead of complaining," he said, "and as a punishment, you can now put on your Witch's hat and tell me what you think of the new Major-Domo I have just engaged."

"I have seen him," Imeldra replied, "and I think you have made a mistake."

"What do you mean by that?" the Earl enquired.

"He is too pleasant, too oily to be trusted," Imeldra answered. "Be careful of him, Papa, or I am quite certain he will cheat you."

Her warning had made the Earl take a little more trouble than usual in observing the new servant's behaviour, and within three weeks he discovered that the man was cheating him and dismissed him.

Yet as far as the Marquis was concerned, Imeldra found herself up against a strangely impenetrable barrier, and it fascinated her.

When after dinner they moved back to the Salon it was to find that the room was warm because the fire had been lit in the polished silver grate.

Instead of sitting formally on the sofa as she had done before, Imeldra sat down on the hearthrug in front of the fire, holding out her hands towards it.

"You are cold?" the Marquis asked.

"I find it very cold in England in the winter," Imeldra answered, "and I sometimes long for the sunshine of Egypt and the warmth of North Africa."

She had spoken without thinking, and the Marquis asked:

"What does your father do that you travel so extensively abroad?"

There was a little pause as Imeldra thought quickly.

"He is an explorer," she said, thinking that in a way this was true as the Earl was always exploring new places.

She also made a mental note to tell William Gladwin what she had said.

"You are not in the least like any explorer's daughter I have seen," the Marquis remarked. "They are usually overhearty young women wearing heavy boots and veils over their topees, to keep out the flies."

Imeldra laughed.

"How do you know I do not look like that when I am not dining in a house like this?"

"Tell me about yourself," the Marquis asked beguilingly, leaning forward towards her.

She looked up at him and thought it was something she would like to do, but she knew that it would not only be indiscreet, but there was every likelihood because of his reputation for correctness that he would force her to leave tomorrow for her grandmother's.

"What do you want to know?" she asked.

"Why you are as you are, and why you are so mysterious about yourself."

"Am I mysterious?" Imeldra questioned. "I thought I had been very frank."

"You have been nothing of the sort," the Marquis said, "and I am well aware that everything you have said has been chosen purposely to bewilder me."

He paused before he continued:

"Talking to you is like stepping into a maze. I think I have found the way, then suddenly I can go no further, and I have to try again. So far I have never ever been near the centre of my objective."

"And what is that?"

"To know you, to understand why you are staying with me and why you look as you do."

Imeldra made a helpless little gesture with her

hands as if it was too hard to explain. Then she said:

"What else?"

"So many questions that it is hard to choose," the Marquis said. "But let me try one. Have you ever been kissed?"

Imeldra's eyes widened. Then she replied:

"Now you are being far too intimate on such a short acquaintance. Suppose I asked you that sort of question about yourself?"

There was a silence before the Marquis said:

"Do you really think it is a short acquaintance? I feel, Imeldra, as if I have known you since the beginning of time. But I thought we would never meet, and that you were only a figment of my imagination and my dreams."

The way he spoke was so different from the way they had talked before when duelling with each other that Imeldra looked up at him in astonishment.

As she did so the Marquis put out his hands and clasping her arms above the elbows drew her forward so that she was kneeling at his feet.

She did not struggle, as it was impossible to do so. Still holding her and looking into her eyes, his face close to hers, he said:

"I think you have bewitched me. What am I to do about it?"

"What do you want to do?"

"You know without my telling you that I want to kiss you," the Marquis answered, "but because you are a guest under my roof, and because I deliberately invited you to dine with me alone, I am trying now to behave in the way which you call 'correct.'"

"Thank you," Imeldra said. "I have never been

kissed . . . and long ago I decided that the only person I would allow to do so would be the man I loved with my whole heart as he loved me."

She spoke softly and although the Marquis was still holding her she was not afraid, but quite sure, although she had no grounds for thinking so, that he would not hurt or upset her.

"That is what I guessed you would think and say," the Marquis said. "How is it possible that we know so much about each other?"

His voice was very deep. Somehow it seemed to strike a chord in Imeldra's heart and she felt her whole being respond to him in a manner she had never known before.

She did not reply, and after a moment he said:

"Tell me what you feel about me. I have to know."

Then as if he compelled her to tell the truth, Imeldra replied:

"I have been puzzling ever since we met as to why you are not happy. You have everything, and yet there is something wrong which affects you deeply, but I feel that I cannot reach it."

The Marquis's fingers tightened on her arms until it was painful. Then suddenly he released her so that she sat back on her heels and he rose to his feet.

"As you say," he said, "there is something wrong, and it is something I have no wish to talk about."

Then in a very different tone of voice which seemed somehow to grate on the air:

"Let me show you my pictures. I am sure you are more interested in them than in anything else."

He walked away from her as he spoke to stand in

front of one by Reynolds which she had admired earlier in the day.

It was one of the Marquis's ancestors wearing the red coat of his Regiment and standing beside his horse.

The Marquis stood looking up at it and Imeldra knew he was not seeing anything but the darkness within his own soul.

She stood in front of the fire and suddenly felt cold, as if he had shut her out and because he had done so she was alone with an emptiness which was like a barren desert.

She did not speak. She only stood looking at him and as she did so she longed to help him.

It was as if every nerve in her body was vibrating towards him because, although he had not said so, he needed her.

The Marquis turned suddenly from his contemplation of the picture and they looked across the room at each other.

For a moment neither of them spoke or moved. Then he said in a voice that seemed to echo around the walls:

"For God's sake do not make it more difficult for me than it is already!"

With that he went from the Salon leaving Imeldra alone.

* * *

Later when Imeldra was in bed she could hardly believe it had happened that the evening had ended so abruptly, and yet she could not sleep for hearing the

pain in the Marquis's voice and knowing he was suffering.

'I can feel it,' she thought to herself, 'I can feel
it in me, and it is almost as though we were one person
rather than two.'

Because the explanation for this was frightening
she tried hard to think of her father, of her mother,
of anything rather than the Marquis, but inescapably
he was there with her.

Imeldra awoke early, thinking that the dramatics
of the night before were ridiculous and she must have
imagined them.

'I am getting in too far,' she thought.

Then she asked why the most simple remarks
should have such an effect on her, and why after they
had laughed and duelled at dinner there had been a
change once they were alone in the Salon.

Because it was impossible to sleep any longer,
Imeldra rose and rang the bell and when Emma appeared sent her to ask if she could have a horse to
ride.

She was almost dressed before Emma reappeared
to say that there would be a horse waiting for her at
the side-door in ten minutes's time.

Quickly Imeldra hurried into her riding-habit, and
only when she had fastened her high-crowned hat
trimmed with a gauze veil securely on her head did
she wonder if whilst riding she would encounter the
Marquis.

She had the feeling he might think it a presumption
that she would wish to ride his horses, then told herself
that after what had happened the night before nothing

unusual that either of them did would seem surprising.

She went to the side-door to find, as she expected, a very well-bred horse waiting for her with a groom to accompany her.

She was helped into the saddle, her full skirts arranged behind the single stirrup, then set off leading the way to the front of the house and into the Park.

The horse responded to her slightest touch and Imeldra knew that she had been given a perfectly trained animal in case she was an inexperienced rider.

As she had ridden her father's horses at home and in many of the countries in which they had travelled, she was not afraid of the most wild or spirited animal.

Because this morning she wanted to think, it was a relief that she did not have to battle with a horse as well as with her own thoughts.

They rode through the Park and the groom told her that on the other side of a fir wood there was the ground where the Marquis's horses were trained.

Imeldra thanked him for the information and rode through a path between the trees, feeling because they were dark and the sun found it hard to percolate through the thickness of their branches that the wood was mysterious and in a way impenetrable like the Marquis.

On the flat ground beyond the wood was a gallop stretching for over a mile.

As soon as she reached it Imeldra just touched her horse with the whip and he set off at a gallop which she felt would clear her mind and perhaps sweep away some of the problems that seemed to be closing in on her.

She was half-way down the gallop when she saw a rider come from between some trees at the side of it, and knew who it was.

She did not pull in her own mount and knew there was no need.

As she reached the Marquis, his own horse leapt forward and they were riding side by side at a wild speed which in itself was an indescribable exhilaration.

They rode faster and faster and only when the end of the gallop was a short way ahead did they pull in their horses.

As they came to a halt, Imeldra turned a laughing face toward the Marquis saying:

"That was wonderful!"

"I somehow knew you would ride as well as you do," he said.

"Just as I knew you would seem part of your horse," she replied without thinking.

It was true. On his huge black stallion with the magnificent head the Marquis seemed in a way she could not describe a better rider even than her father, who was exceptional.

He might have been a god who had ridden down from Olympus to be amongst the human race.

The Marquis must have been following her thoughts for he said a little wryly:

"Exactly! And if I have come from Olympus, so have you!"

"How did you know that was what I was thinking?"

"In the same way that you read my thoughts," he answered.

"But I cannot read them all."

"I expect you will also have secrets from me," he said, "but I shall try to prevent that from happening."

Imeldra did not reply, and after a moment he said:

"I was expecting to see you later this morning and intended to apologise for my behaviour. I have no excuse except that it is a secret that cannot be told at the moment, if ever. All I can ask is that you will forgive me, and we can continue where we left off at dinner."

Imeldra glanced at him from under her eyelashes and they both turned their horses to walk slowly back along the gallop in the direction from which they had come.

"You have not answered me," the Marquis said after a moment.

"I am wondering what to say."

"Leave everything to me," he said. "There are so many things I want to show you, so much about which I want to talk to you, and I am only afraid you may leave me in the same inexplicable manner in which you arrived."

"Was it really so inexplicable?" Imeldra asked, thinking that William Gladwin was supposed to be her grandfather.

"Completely and utterly inexplicable," the Marquis answered firmly.

Because she thought it wiser not to argue Imeldra asked:

"What do you plan to show me first?"

"A million things," he answered, "which may take a million years. But as it is a fine day, shall we start with the Folly which was erected for my great-grandmother?"

"That sounds very exciting," Imeldra said with a little lilt in her voice.

"We will drive there," the Marquis said, "and as it takes a little time, could you be ready at eleven-thirty? And we will take our luncheon with us."

She flashed him a smile that seemed to have caught the sunlight.

"It is something I should adore to do."

"Then that is arranged," he said and she knew he was pleased. "And to celebrate it I will race you to the end of the gallop."

The Marquis won by a length, and Imeldra told herself it was because his horse was superior and larger than hers, but she knew also that he was such an exceptional rider that there was every likelihood of his winning on any horse, however indifferent.

Because at the end of the gallop the groom was waiting, the Marquis raised his hat and said formally:

"I expect Jim will take you back through the woods where there is a very pleasant ride down to the house. Good day for the moment, Miss Gladwin."

"Goodbye, My Lord," Imeldra replied.

As he rode away she felt a little piqued because he was leaving her.

Then she was sure that his reason for doing so was to ensure that the groom did not carry back tales to the stables of how they had met, and he was in fact protecting her against the gossip of his servants.

But she told herself that was ridiculous, considering they had dined together and he was taking her driving this afternoon.

There was also the possibility that he might not

wish to see too much of her, and yet she was sure that was not the reason.

'He is very mysterious,' she thought, and could not prevent herself thinking of him the whole way she was riding back to the house.

*   *   *

It was a delight that Imeldra found it hard to put into words to be driving in the high Phaeton with its large wheels behind a superb pair of chestnuts alone with the Marquis.

She had been surprised when she came downstairs wearing one of her prettiest gowns with a chip-straw bonnet trimmed with a wreath of cornflowers to find they were not to be accompanied by a groom.

As they drove away with a large picnic-basket in the back of the Phaeton, almost as if she had asked the question the Marquis said:

"I have had these horses ever since they were born and I helped to train them. They will come when I call them, and I feel that when I am driving them there is no need for me to bring a groom with me."

"How did you know that was what I wanted to know?" Imeldra asked.

He did not reply, and because she knew it was now so obvious that they could reach each other's thoughts, any explanation was superfluous.

"Will you show me your stables?" she asked.

"I am only surprised you have not inspected them already!"

"You forget I only arrived yesterday."

As she spoke she felt as if she had already been here for years and the Marquis was part of her life.

Then she told herself she was being absurd.

It was only because while she was away at School, she had not met all the interesting and exciting men that were always around her father, that the Marquis was making such an impact upon her.

"Also I am older," Imeldra reasoned, "and therefore a man obviously means more to me than men did when I was just a School-girl."

Yet some very astute part of her brain was arguing that this was not true, and already there was a closeness between herself and the Marquis which could not be explained away logically or reasonably.

"When I saw you first thing this morning," the Marquis said with his eyes on his horses's heads, "I thought you were even lovelier than you were yesterday, but now I know that you are even more beautiful than you were this morning."

Because his voice was low and intimate, Imeldra felt a strange feeling in her heart and because unaccountably she felt a little shy she said quickly:

"Somebody told me that you were very reserved, but that pretty speech makes me think they were mistaken."

"Shall I tell you that it is very unusual for me to make pretty speeches?" the Marquis asked, "Or are you aware of that already?"

He did not wait for Imeldra to answer, but asked:

"Did you think of me last night?"

"Did you expect me to do anything else?" she replied.

"I do not mean about the way I behaved for which

I have already apologised, but of me, as a man?"

"It would be very difficult for me not to do so."

"You sound as if you tried."

"I tried, of course I tried," Imeldra answered. "I like puzzles but not when I find them too difficult to solve."

"So that is what you are trying to do," the Marquis said. "Well, please stop whatever you are doing."

"Why?"

"Because it would be a very great mistake for you to solve the puzzle of the Marquis of Marizon."

"In saying things like that you must be aware that it makes me determined not only to solve your puzzle, but also to help you."

The Marquis gave a short laugh that had no humour in it.

"It is utterly and completely impossible for you to do that."

"Can you tell me why?"

"No!"

Imeldra gave a little cry.

"You are making it very difficult for me."

"Why should it be difficult?" the Marquis asked in an almost irritated voice. "And why do you want to talk of things that do not concern you?"

He paused for a moment before he went on:

"The whole thing is ridiculous. As your host I am attempting to entertain a very attractive young lady who is staying uninvited in my house. Why can you not be a quite ordinary young woman and enjoy it . . ."

". . . and of course," Imeldra interrupted, "feel flattered and honoured by your condescension."

"That is definitely not the sort of remark a young

woman should make to me," the Marquis said.

"And as a conventional young woman, if she was lucky enough to be entertained by the noble Marquis on one occasion, she would certainly not be invited a second time," Imeldra said.

"You cannot be sure of that. I might find her very entertaining."

"I doubt it, and after she had goggled at you because she was so impressed by your appearance, and your title, you would find yourself longing to be with the sophisticated beauties you have left behind in London."

The Marquis laughed.

"How do you know I have left sophisticated beauties behind in London?"

Imeldra thought she could tell him a great deal about the beauties with whom her father had spent so much of his time, and also she suspected that the women who pursued him in London were very much the same as those who had chased him in Paris, in Rome and anywhere else in the world to which they had travelled.

But she thought to say too much would be revealing, and she therefore said in an effort to prevent the Marquis from questioning her too closely:

"How often has Your Lordship been in love?"

He took his eyes off the horses to look at her before he replied:

"Will you believe me if I give you the truthful answer?"

"That depends upon what it is."

"Then if we are speaking of love as I think you mean it, the answer is 'never!'"

"Why should the way I think of love be any different from anybody's else's?"

"Because I an quite certain," the Marquis said, "that for you, coming from Olympus, love is an ideal, an ecstasy with silver wings carried on the music of the spheres."

He spoke in a way which made Imeldra draw in her breath, and she knew that it was exactly what she had thought love would be like.

It was the love which her father and mother had known and the love she sought for herself.

Because she had no answer ready they drove for a long way in silence. Then ahead of them she saw a strange monument not unlike the Leaning Tower of Pisa silhouetted against the sky.

"Is that the Folly?" she asked.

"Perhaps it is the wrong word for it," the Marquis replied. "It is a memorial of love, a Temple erected by my great-grandfather whose heart was broken when his wife died."

"Like the Taj Mahal," Imeldra murmured.

"Exactly!"

"That is the ideal love," Imeldra said.

"Of course!" the Marquis agreed. "And the men who erected such monuments had experienced the love of which we were just speaking."

"The love which you have never known," Imeldra added.

The Marquis did not answer, and as she looked at him she thought that the lines of cynicism on his face were deep in the sunlight.

She thought too, although she was not certain, that his eyes were as hard and dark as they had been when she had first seen him.

chapter four

HAVING eaten a delicious luncheon, Imeldra looked about her.

She thought the Temple was like no building she had ever seen before.

Inside it was circular partly Grecian in style, partly Moslem with stone filigree windows that let in the sunlight to make strange patterns on the marble floor.

There was a raised dais, again circular, in the centre on which was a statue of Pan dancing as he played his reed pipes.

Imeldra and the Marquis were sitting against the plinth of the statue, with their picnic basket in front of them. Through the open door there was an exquisite view stretching out over the valley.

It was so unusual, and at the same time so romantic that Imeldra felt as if she had stepped into another world, and there was strange music playing around them.

This was partially due to the wind which made melodious sounds as it blew through the dome of the building which rose high towards the sky so that it could be seen for miles around.

But it was also, she thought, music which came from within her and the Marquis because they were so closely attuned to each other.

Because the building in which they were sitting was mystical and at the same time dedicated to love, the Marquis's voice seemed to deepen when he spoke to her, and she found it hard to look at him in case he should see the expression in her eyes.

At first they talked of ordinary things, but there were strange silences when it seemed as if her heart was talking to his, and there was no need for words.

Now the Marquis leaned back against the stone to say:

"Somehow you seem to fit in here as if you belonged not to this generation, but to the past."

"All the same...I am looking forward to the...future," Imeldra replied.

"That I can understand, but for me there is no future."

He spoke almost as if he was talking to himself, and Imeldra gave a little cry.

"What do you mean? How can you say such a thing?"

"It is something I should not have said because you would not understand."

"But I want to understand. You know I want

to . . . understand and as I have already said . . . to help you."

"You have done that already by letting me know you exist and are what I have been looking for, although I was not aware of it."

The way he spoke made her look away from him out through the open door to the sunshine of the valley beneath them.

As she did so her profile was silhouetted against the white marble of the building, and because she had taken off her bonnet while they ate luncheon, the sunshine on her hair made it seem as if there were little flames flickering on her head.

"How can you be so beautiful?" the Marquis asked. "How is it possible for any woman in this age and day to look like you?"

"The answer to that is very simple," Imeldra answered. "I was born to two people who loved each other completely and idealistically, as your great-grandfather must have loved the woman for whom he built this Temple."

"And you think that love is beautiful?" the Marquis asked.

"Of course it is," Imeldra answered. "How could it be anything else? The world was made with love and for love and it is only men who have made it ugly."

She thought as she spoke of her father running away with Lady Bullington, whom he did not love in the same way that he had loved his wife, and felt that was an ugly love—a love which was concerned only with the body and not the mind and soul.

She had forgotten that the Marquis was watching her and after a moment he asked:

"What are you thinking about? Who has hurt you? Who has dared to make you unhappy?"

She did not reply and he added:

"If it is a man I will want to kill him!"

The violence with which he spoke startled her and she turned to look at him in surprise.

For a moment they stared at each other. Then the Marquis rose and walked down the steps from the dais towards the open door.

Imeldra was afraid that he was about to leave her as he had done last night, and she followed him.

As she reached him to stand beside him, she said:

"You are torturing yourself. Why can you not tell . . . me what is . . . wrong?"

He turned towards her and now his eyes were dark with pain and because she could not bear him to suffer in such a way she put her hands palm downwards on his chest and looking up at him, pleaded:

"Tell me . . . please . . . tell me . . . I want so desperately to . . . help you."

"Why?"

Imeldra sought for an answer and knew what it was.

Somehow she should have expected it, and yet at the same time she had shied away from it because it was too big, too overwhelming to contemplate.

Yet she knew the truth, even while her lips would not frame the words.

Once again the Marquis was reading her thoughts.

Very quietly so that it was almost a whisper on the wind, he said:

"You love me!"

Imeldra drew in her breath.

Then with a sound that was half one of exaltation and half of pain he put his arms around her and his lips came down on hers.

As he touched her, Imeldra knew that this was real love, the love she had felt for him ever since she had seen him and perhaps in an eternity before they had met each other again.

It was the love she had always believed would be hers, and yet was afraid she would not find it.

Now as the Marquis's lips held hers captive she felt an ecstacy which was vaguely familiar because it had been in her dreams, rising within her until it became an unbelievable rapture.

It was so glorious, so perfect, that it was the divine ideal of which they had spoken, and which was love in all its glory and perfection.

The Marquis drew her closer and still closer and his lips became possessive, demanding, passionate, yet at the same time there was a tenderness she did not expect from him.

It was as if because she was infinitely precious she knew he would not hurt her.

He kissed her until the Temple vanished and with it the world outside, and there was only the light of the gods and the music which joined them together and carried them higher and still higher towards the Divine.

Only when the wonder of it and the ecstasy became almost too much to bear, did Imeldra give a little murmur and hide her face against the Marquis's neck.

He did not move but his arms seemed to give her

a security and safety she had never known before.

Only after a long while did he say in a voice hoarse, unsteady and almost unrecognisable:

"I love you and there is nothing and nobody in the world except you!"

Imeldra drew in her breath.

"That is what I . . . feel. I have . . . known you for many . . . many years . . . and that is why we . . . think alike . . . and feel . . . alike."

The Marquis did not answer. He merely turned her face up to his, and was kissing her again.

Now his kisses were different and she knew with a sudden fear that he was kissing her frantically, fiercely, because he thought he must lose her.

Yet it was impossible to think because the fire of the Marquis's kisses awoke an answering flame within herself to ignite a fire which possessed her.

It was inescapable, but at the same time, as she knew he felt the same, it was a fire purified by love. What they felt for each other was very human, and yet part of God.

Only when they were both breathless did the Marquis say in a voice that was broken and hoarse:

"How can I lose you? How can I let you go? You are mine, Imeldra, mine with every breath you draw, with every thought you think."

Because she believed that too, the agony in his voice frightened her and she asked:

"Why . . . must you . . . lose me?"

He looked down at her, staring at her face as if he would engrave it on his memory for ever. Then he said:

"Because I cannot marry you."

She stiffened and it flashed through her mind that because of his rank and prestige he would not lower himself to marry a social inferior; the granddaughter of a man whom he paid for his services.

There was no need to put into words what she was thinking for the Marquis saw it in her eyes and he said angrily:

"How dare you think such a thing! Do you really imagine that is the reason why I cannot ask you to be my wife? If you were born in the gutter, or were the daughter of a crossing-sweeper, I would go down on my knees and beg you to honour me by giving me your hand in marriage. But that is something I cannot do."

"Why . . . not?"

"That is what I cannot tell you," the Marquis replied, "but because there is a reason, you have to go away."

Imeldra felt as if an icy hand clutched her heart, but she managed to say:

"Suppose I . . . refuse? Suppose I . . . insist . . . on staying here . . . with or . . . without . . . marriage?"

Her voice trembled on the words and she saw the bitter smile that crossed the Marquis's face.

"Do you suppose I have not thought of that?" he asked. "Do you suppose I did not lie awake last night enduring all the temptations of St. Anthony rolled into one?"

He pulled her so close to him that she could hardly breathe as he went on:

"Oh, my precious little goddess, of course I have thought of how we might be together, but I have not yet sunk to such depths of depravity that I would spoil anything so perfect, so pure or so unbelievably beautiful."

Because the way he spoke moved her so tremendously, Imeldra felt the tears come into her eyes.

She did not hide them but went on looking at the Marquis, knowing from the expression on his face that he was being crucified by his own emotions.

"I love you!" he said. "I love you as I never believed it possible to love anybody. You fill my whole world, you are like a light in the darkness which is destroying me."

"But I am . . . alive," Imeldra replied, "and perhaps I can lead you out of the . . . darkness and we can be . . . happy."

He shook his head and she felt as if he quenched the fire that burnt within her, leaving nothing but ashes.

"You must go away, my lovely one," he said. "Forget me, and one day you will find a man who will love you as I do and, although I cannot bear to think of it, you will marry him."

"That will never happen," Imeldra replied, "because now I know that I love you and . . . belong to you . . . I shall never . . . let another man . . . touch me."

"You think that now," the Marquis said, "but you are very young, and the young forget."

"Will you forget?"

"That is different. I am old, not in years, but in bitterness and hatred and despair."

"How can you talk like that?" Imeldra asked. "How can you throw away anything so wonderful and glorious as our love for each other?"

He did not answer and she went on:

"It is as wrong as if you knocked down this exquisite memorial to your great-grandmother. It is as wrong as if you burnt Marizon to the ground with all the beauty it contains. What we have been given is a gift from God, and neither of us can refuse it."

"That is the sort of thing you would say, my darling," the Marquis said tenderly, "but because you yourself come from God, because I want to kneel at your feet and pray for your happiness, I know that I have to leave you."

"Why? Why?" Imeldra cried. "What have you done? What crime have you committed that love cannot understand and . . . forgive?"

As if he had no words in which to answer her the Marquis drew her close to him and kissed her again.

Now there was no fire on his lips only, she thought, a kind of dull misery, as if his despair had left him cold, and she no longer had the power to excite him.

Then he released her and said in a voice of authority which she felt she must obey:

"Pack up the picnic things while I collect the horses."

When he had spoken he walked outside leaving her standing looking after him.

She wanted to scream, to cry, to plead with him on her knees to tell her what was wrong and make her understand. But she knew it would be no use.

Because she loved him so desperately she knew that for the moment he was driven almost beyond endurance.

Then as he walked away to where the horses were grazing a little below them, she felt as if he was not a masterful man, but a little boy—as if he were her son—who was caught up in events too deep and too frightening for him to understand and which menaced him to the point where he could find no escape.

Because it was the only way she could help him, she began to pray.

"Save him...God. Save him from whatever it is that is...making him so...unhappy. Let us be together. Do not leave us...alone and...crippled without...each other...please, God...please."

Automatically, because the Marquis had ordered it, she put the plates and glasses they had used back into the picnic-basket and shut down the lid.

But all the time she was praying, feeling that if she could find no answer to the Marquis's secret, then it would be known to God, and He would be the only person who could solve it.

* * *

Driving back in the sunshine her prayers turned from God to her mother.

She felt as if she needed her more than she had ever needed her since she had died.

Only her mother would understand the love that was pulsating through her for the man who said she must go away.

Only her mother would understand how he filled her whole world, the whole sky, and if she lost him she would have lost everything that mattered including the very joy of living.

"Make him love me, Mama, so that nothing else...matters," she pleaded. "Make him love me enough to confide in me, and when he does so show me how I can . . . guide and . . . inspire him as . . . you did Papa."

She was praying so intensely that she gave a little start when the Marquis, who had been looking ahead with a frown between his eyes, turned to look at her.

"Take off your glove and give me your hand," he said. "I have to touch you."

The way he spoke made her feel as if the dark cloud had for the moment lifted.

Obediently she undid the buttons on her long gloves and started to pull off the one from her right hand.

As if she was not quick enough for him the Marquis drew it from her fingers, thrust it into his pocket, then clasped her hand in his.

"Now I am touching you again, and we are one," he said almost beneath his breath.

"And our vibrations are joined," Imeldra added, "as they were the very first time we met."

He made a little sound that was half a laugh.

"I thought the same, and when you turned from the picture to look at me it was as if you were bathed in light and the rays came towards me as if they were alive."

"Oh, darling, how can we . . . escape each other?" Imeldra asked.

The Marquis's fingers tightened on hers until his clasp was painful.

"Say that to me again!" he begged. "Say it with that little note in your voice which will always haunt me and prevent me from hearing anything any other woman will ever say to me."

"Darling . . . darling . . . darling . . . I love . . . you!" Imeldra whispered.

The Marquis, with his eyes on the road in front of them, raised her hand.

He kissed her fingers, then his lips lingered on the softness of her skin.

Even with one hand he was still driving superbly, and she thought because he was touching her the light he had spoken of which emanated from them both, seemed to vibrate around them.

Instinctively she moved a little closer to him and for a moment laid her cheek against his arm.

Because she was half-afraid that when they reached Marizon he would vanish without saying any more to her, she asked:

"May I dine with you tonight?"

"I ought to say 'no.'"

"Please say . . . yes. There are still so many . . . things we have to say to . . . each other."

As she spoke she had the frantic feeling that time was running out, and at any moment he would be gone and she would never see him again.

She knew without his telling her so that he would leave her at Marizon. Because he thought she wanted to be with her grandfather, he would go away.

If that happened, she knew she would go at once to her grandmother because she could not bear the great house which would be an empty shell without him.

'I must treasure every moment,' she thought frantically, 'every second I am with him, and in the long years ahead they will be something to remember.'

Then it suddenly struck her that in the same circumstances her father would not give in, but would fight for what he wanted.

He had always won whatever he set his heart on, and it was only death that had defeated him, when he lost the treasure he had prized above all others.

In all other difficulties he had always fought until he was the victor, and Imeldra knew that was what she must do too.

Something proud and resolute rose within her, and she told herself she would not lose the Marquis.

Somehow, however difficult it might be, she would find out what was wrong, and if it was possible she would put it right.

Right or wrong, she would stay with him. He was hers and she was his, and love was greater than social barriers, than crime, or every sin in the calendar.

"I will not be defeated," she swore, but her instinct told her this was something she should not tell him at this moment.

Instead she said softly:

"Let us dine together and pretend that nothing is wrong! That we are just two people who have . . . fallen in love and found that they have . . . reached a Heaven . . . they did not even think . . . existed."

The Marquis did not speak and she felt he was hesitating, so she added quickly:

"Please . . . let us do . . . that. It would be like a . . . present which you would give me . . . and I would . . . give you."

"A present, my precious!" the Marquis said softly. "You know, if it was possible, I would like to drape you in diamonds, cover you in sables, and you would never want for anything in your whole life that I would not provide."

"Instead I want something far more valuable . . . a

few...hours with you," Imeldra said. "Hours that will sparkle like the...stars in the sky...and when you...kiss me I know that you will...take me up to them and we will no longer be on...earth."

She spoke very softly, and the Marquis released her hand for a moment as he turned the horses round a rather difficult corner.

When he had done so he said:

"You shall have your present, my beautiful one, I promise you that, and for today at least, we will not think of tomorrow."

"Thank you," Imeldra said, and once again she laid her cheek against his arm.

All too soon Marizon came in sight. For once its grandeur and beauty had no appeal for Imeldra, and instead it was a prison in which the Marquis was chained by some secret he would not reveal.

She knew when tomorrow came she might have to go away because she was the intruder.

Then as they drew up outside the steps she told herself she would fight and go on fighting and not until she had died, would she give up.

A footman helped her down from the Phaeton, a groom ran to the horses's heads and she and the Marquis walked up the steps side by side.

Without speaking, almost as if they instinctively knew what the other wanted, they walked across the Hall and into the Study where Imeldra had learned the Marquis habitually sat when he was alone.

It was an attractive room hung with pictures of horses and dogs, and so essentially masculine that it was a perfect background for him.

As the footman shut the door behind them they

moved to the middle of the room, then stopped and looked at each other.

"I expect there are a great many things I ought to do," the Marquis said, "but first, my darling, because this is part of your present, I have to kiss you."

"That is what I am . . . waiting to . . . receive," Imeldra whispered.

She lifted her face to his and he undid the ribbons of her bonnet to fling it down on the sofa.

Then he touched her hair as if smoothing it into place, but in reality feeling the silkiness of it with his fingers.

Then slowly, as if he savoured the moment, his lips found hers.

It was so perfect, so lovely that once again Imeldra felt there was music and they were enveloped with the love they felt for each other.

He kissed her until the room seemed to swim dizzily round them and she felt they were flying up towards the stars.

Then there was the sound of the door opening and they only just had time to move apart before the Butler announced:

"Excuse me, M'Lord, but I forgot to tell you there's somebody to see you—on business."

"I expect it is one of the farmers," the Marquis said to Imeldra.

His eyes rested on her lips for a moment and she felt as if he kissed her again.

Then as if he forced himself to behave correctly in front of a servant he walked to the door and she heard him moving a little way down the passage.

He asked the Butler where his visitor was, and he

told him in the Morning-Room, which Imeldra knew was situated almost opposite to where she was now.

Then as she stood listening she suddenly remembered that in his pocket the Marquis had placed her glove.

Because he was so punctilious in front of the staff she thought perhaps it would be embarrassing when he undressed if his valet discovered it.

Without thinking, except that she might save him any embarrassment, she ran from the Study along the passage just as the Marquis was entering the Morning-Room.

The Butler had actually shut the door behind him and because she realised it was too late, Imeldra stopped and said a little lamely:

"I thought I would get a book from the Library."

The Library was next to the Morning-Room and the Butler opened the door for her.

She thanked him and went inside carrying her bonnet, thinking she would take a book—any book would do for she would not read it—and go upstairs.

Even as she walked further into the Library she heard the Marquis's voice raised in anger and realised that as in most houses built in that period State Rooms all connected with each other.

Her mother had often laughed and said that at Kingsclere they really lived in a passage.

It suddenly struck Imeldra that there was a chance that the visitor, whose name the Butler had not announced, might be connected in some way with the Marquis's secret.

There was no reason for her to think such a thing

or that there was anything unusual in someone calling to see the Marquis on business.

It was only her special perceptiveness which brought the idea to her mind, and then her instinct made her sure it was true.

Without considering whether or not she was eavesdropping, she walked down the Library to the door at the end of it, and when she reached it she saw that it was not completely closed and it was quite easy to hear what was being said in the next room.

It was even easier than it might have been because the Marquis was speaking loudly and angrily.

"How dare you come here, Jolie!" he said. "If you wish to communicate with me you can write, or I can give you the name of my Solicitors."

"And what would your answer have been?" a woman replied. "Besides it would be a mistake to put into writing what I have to say to you."

As she spoke Imeldra realised that while her English was good she spoke with a slightly foreign accent.

"We have nothing to say to each other," the Marquis replied sharply. "When I accepted your blackmailing terms and gave you £25,000, you promised to keep out of my life as long as I kept to the conditions you imposed upon me. I have done that, and I have nothing more to say."

The woman to whom he was speaking gave a little laugh and it was not a pleasant sound.

"Money does not last for ever! In five years it shrinks and shrinks until—poof!—it has disappeared!"

"By that I presume you have been gambling," the Marquis said in a hard voice. "Well, you can find somebody else's money to gamble with. I have no intention of giving you any more."

"In which case I must bring your brother to England to plead with you," the Frenchwoman said softly, "or shall I ask for justice in the Courts?"

There was silence for a moment. Then the Marquis said sharply:

"We have been through all this before. I gave you £25,000 and my word of honour that I would not marry on condition that you made no further claims upon me or my title."

Imeldra drew in her breath. She felt that the Frenchwoman shrugged her shoulders before she said:

"Have you any idea what it is like to grow old when you have been beautiful and famous? Once people queued outside the Theatre from first thing in the morning so that they could hear me sing. I received not only bouquets but jewels from Kings, Emperors, Princes, and of course a Marquis!"

She gave a deep sigh before she went on:

"Mais maintenant pauvre Jolie is no longer young and beautiful, and the only places where I can sing are the Cafés and the low Cabarets. So I am poor, while you are rich. Think how comfortable I would be if I were living here with my son."

"Which you are not," the Marquis said briefly.

"If I showed my papers, and as you know they are very safe in my Bank in Paris, to the English Justices, this is where I would be, and André would be in your place."

Imeldra drew in her breath. For the moment she could hardly sort out in her mind the whole impact of what she had heard, but she had to go on listening.

"What I want, *mon cher Marquis,*" the French-woman said, and the way she said his title was a sneer, "is enough money to be comfortable and not be dependent upon earning my living as I have done all my life. And money of course for André, who is bored with counting his pennies when he might be a rich English Lord."

"I trusted you when you said you would not trouble me again," the Marquis answered, "but presumably I was mistaken. If I give you more money what will you do? Throw it away on the gaming tables?"

"Why should I not have my fun as you have yours?" the woman demanded.

There was silence and she added:

"If you do not give me what I want, I will instruct the best Lawyer in Paris to take my papers and my petition to the House of Lords. Think of the scandal, and when I win my case I will perhaps be generous to you, or perhaps not."

"Damn you!" the Marquis exclaimed.

But he spoke dully as if he could not fight the woman who was taunting him.

There was the sound of his footsteps crossing the room.

"I will fetch my cheque-book," he said. "Stay here and do not dare to speak to anybody in my household. If you do, I swear I will let you bring a case against me and I'll face the consequences."

He did not wait for the Frenchwoman to answer,

but went out of the Morning-Room slamming the door behind him.

Imeldra was aware that he crossed the passage to his Study where doubtless he would find the cheque-book in his desk.

She heard the woman in the next room give a low, unpleasant laugh as of somebody who had gained her objective, before she began to hum a popular French song.

It was then Imeldra knew that she must think over what she had heard and consider what her next move should be before she let the Marquis become aware that she had learnt his secret.

She waiting in the Library until she heard him return and she thought his footsteps seemed slow as if he had suddenly aged in the interval.

She heard him cross the room to the table by the window and say in a voice that was hard and cold:

"I will give you £10,000 and not a penny more!"

"Fifteen!" the Frenchwoman insisted.

"Ten! As it is I am bleeding the estate of money that was destined for people who are in greater need than you."

"You can always sell one of your pictures," *Madame* Jolie replied. "I have read about them even in the Paris newspapers."

"The pictures are entailed to the son that you have made sure I shall never have," the Marquis retorted bitterly.

The Frenchwoman laughed.

"Oo, la, la! There are plenty of women to amuse you, and marriage is not always a bed of roses, as I myself have discovered."

"£10,000 will keep you comfortable for a long time."

"That depends—that very much depends," *Madame* Jolie answered.

Imeldra realised that she was taunting the Marquis again and because she could bear no more, swiftly and silently she ran down the Library to the door which led into the passage.

She opened it and then she was running, as if all the devils of Hell were pursuing her, up to the sanctuary of her bedroom in the East Wing.

Only when she had flung herself down on the bed to think did she realise what she had overheard, and the horror of it.

For a moment it seemed impossible, and then as the puzzle fell into place she understood now all too clearly that the Marquis was not the Marquis.

He had an elder brother, the son of a French singer, and it was André who should have inherited Marizon.

For the moment she could hardly credit that the old Marquis, who had been the height of propriety, who had disapproved of her father and after her mother's death had refused to have anything to do with him, could have a son whom he did not acknowledge, by a French singer.

It meant of course that the present Marquis's mother had not been legitimately married to his father, if the Frenchwoman was justified in claiming to be the legal wife of the old Marquis.

It was so frightening to think of it that it took a little time for Imeldra to understand exactly what the whole story entailed.

Then she could realise all too clearly why the Marquis had not only allowed himself to be blackmailed, but had even agreed to *Madame* Jolie's stipulation that he should not marry.

It made her hold over him more complete, since if the Marquis did challenge her contention that she was his father's legal wife, his case might be stronger, if he had a family to support his claim, to the title and the estates.

At the same time, even if the Marquis were confident of winning his case if *Madame* Jolie did bring her claim before the House of Lords, nevertheless Imeldra was sure that he would submit to any demands rather than allow the reputation of his father and mother to be pilloried as it would be by the ensuing publicity.

Now at last she could understand why he was cynical and bitter, and why he found little pleasure in the insecurity of his position.

"Oh, darling...darling!" her heart cried out to him. "I must help...you! I must...save you!"

But how, she had no idea!

A knock on the door made her start and she hastily rose from the bed on which she had thrown herself, and walked to the window before she said: "Come in!"

It was Emma.

"There's a note for you, Miss. It's bin brought by a carriage that's waiting by the side-door."

"A carriage?" Imeldra exclaimed.

She knew the only person who would send a message for her would be Mr. Dutton and she wondered what could have occurred, unless in some way her grandmother had been told where she was.

Then she was sure that was impossible and quickly opened the note.

It was written on Kingsclere writing paper and she read:

Dear Lady Imeldra,

It is with deep regret that I have to inform you that your father has been involved in an accident in which he has been badly injured.

He is being brought home today and I am sure you will wish to be here when he arrives.

I have therefore sent the carriage for you, and look forward to seeing you within an hour or so. That will be about the time His Lordship will be here.

I remain, My Lady,
Your most respectful and humble servant,
Richard Dutton.

With a strangled little cry Imeldra said:

"Emma! Quickly! Pack everything I possess! It does not matter how you do so, but I have to leave immediately!"

As if Emma knew by the frantic note in her voice how urgent it was, she fetched two other housemaids and her trunks were brought from the cupboard near her bed-room where they had been stowed.

Almost before Imeldra could change into her travelling-gown her clothes were in the trunks, and the footmen were carrying them downstairs.

She was in such a hurry that it was only when she was ready to leave that she remembered William Gladwin should be told, and also the Marquis.

As she thought of the latter her heart seemed to turn over in her breast, but she knew that for the moment at any rate, he must take second place to the needs of her father.

The footmen were carrying her trunks to the waiting carriage not down the Grand Staircase, but by one that would take them to the side entrance.

"Listen, Emma," she said, "go and tell my grandfather, Mr. Gladwin, as soon as I have left, that I have to go home because my father has had an accident. Do you understand?"

"Yes, o'course, M'Lady."

Imeldra hesitated as to whether she should send a message to the Marquis.

Then she thought it would be a mistake. If he questioned William Gladwin, he would tell him why she had gone, and she doubted if after what they had said to each other today, he would be surprised.

"Thank you for looking after me," she said to Emma.

She gave the girl a guinea which made her eyes light up with excitement, then running to catch up with the footmen ahead of her, Imeldra hurried towards the secondary staircase.

It was only as the carriage from Kingsclere drove down the drive and she looked back at Marizon that the tears came into her eyes.

"Goodbye . . . my love!" she whispered to the Marquis.

Even though she must leave, she was aware that however much her father needed her, she had left her heart behind.

chapter five

ALL the way back to Kingsclere, Imeldra was willing
the horses to hurry, feeling every time they slowed
down for a bend in the road, that she might be too
late for her father.

She could not imagine what kind of accident he
had had or how it had happened, but the knowledge
that he was injured made her afraid in a way she had
never been before.

It was enough to lose him by his having to go
abroad, but if he died and she lost him altogether she
would be utterly and completely alone.

It was as if tragedy after tragedy was piling up on
her, so that for the moment she could sort out none
of her problems, feeling only as if they crushed her
into the ground and everything was dark.

"Hurry! Hurry!" she wanted to call out to Baker,

who was driving with his usual skill but taking no chances.

It was always dangerous on the narrow twisting lanes where it would be impossible to pass without great difficulty a carriage or a cart coming in the opposite direction.

Imeldra tried to puzzle out if that was what had happened to her father, but if as she had suspected, he was driving Lady Bullington to Dover to cross the Channel, they would have been on the main Highway and in that case would have been safer than she was at the moment.

It was however impossible to imagine exactly what had occurred, and she could only pray that her father was not as badly injured as Mr. Dutton had said.

In any case, whatever had happened to him, she knew that she must nurse him and that he would want her by his side.

It was actually less than an hour before the horses turned in at the lodge-gates of Kingsclere, but it seemed to Imeldra as if a hundred years had passed since she had read Mr. Dutton's note.

She tried to keep her mind entirely on her father, but it was almost as if the Marquis was beside her, also needing her help. She wondered frantically how she could save him but there was no answer to that.

Kingsclere looked warm and familiar, and it was a relief when the horses drew up outside the front door to see Mr. Dutton standing on the steps. She knew before he told her that her father had not yet arrived.

"What has happened? Tell me about Papa!" she

asked insistently as she took Mr. Dutton's hand in hers.

"I'm so glad to see you, My Lady," Mr. Dutton replied. "Come and sit down, and I'll tell you everything I know."

Imeldra walked through the Hall and into the Drawing-Room, and she noticed that when Mr. Dutton followed her he left the door open so that he could listen for the sound of the carriage arriving that would bring her father home.

Her face was very pale and her eyes anxious as she said:

"How did you learn about Papa's accident?"

"One of the outriders who was accompanying him to Dover was sent here by the Doctor who attended him after the accident."

"What happened?"

"The outrider, Jason, whom I think you will remember, said it was in no way your father's fault."

"That is what I had supposed," Imeldra said beneath her breath.

"He was driving fast with four horses, but with his usual expertise," Mr. Dutton went on. "He was on a narrow stretch of the Highway when a Stage Coach driven by a drunken driver, who the outrider understood later had had a bet with some of the passengers on the roof that he would reach Dover in record time, came out of a side turning."

Imeldra clasped her hands together. She knew that accidents often happened because the passengers on the Stage Coaches plied the drivers with drink, and then incited them to try to break records.

It invariably meant that the horses were whipped all the way to their destination, which was not only a cruel practice but excessively dangerous.

"According to Jason," Mr. Dutton continued, "His Lordship, by a superb piece of driving, saved his own horses from a head-on collision with the Stage Coach, which drove straight into the Phaeton, partially overturning it against some trees at the side of the road."

Imeldra gave a little gasp and Mr. Dutton lowered his voice as he said:

"Your father was badly crushed and the Lady with whom he was travelling was killed!"

Imeldra put her hands up to her eyes and there was silence before she asked in a voice that trembled:

"But . . . Papa is still . . . alive?"

"When Jason left him he was in such pain," Mr. Dutton said, "that the Doctor gave him laudanum to render him unconscious. But before he did so, your father had given his orders."

"What were they?"

"Jason was a little vague about the Lady who was killed, but he told me he thought His Lordship had given directions as to where her body was to be carried. Then he ordered the servants who were with him and who fortunately received only minor injuries to see that he was brought home."

"Who was with him besides Jason?" Imeldra asked.

"Ben was the other outrider, and there was a groom on the back of the Phaeton but Jason was not sure of his name."

Mr. Dutton paused before he added:

"His Lordship's valet Danvers was just behind in a travelling chariot which contained the luggage."

"I am glad Danvers was with him," Imeldra murmured.

"So am I," Mr. Dutton said, "Danvers is as good a Nurse as any we are likely to obtain, and I am well aware, Lady Imeldra, there are none available in this neighbourhood."

Imeldra knew that was true.

Nursing was confined to the few Nuns who as Little Sisters of the Poor did what they could in London and the big towns, and there were no Nursing Convents, as there were in France.

Otherwise the only women who could be placed in that category were the village Midwives, who were usually hard gin-drinkers and not the sort of creatures her mother would have allowed in the house.

"I will nurse Papa," she said firmly, "and I know that Danvers and our own staff will help me."

"Of course they will," Mr. Dutton replied. "That is exactly what I thought Your Ladyship would wish."

At the same time there was a note in his voice which told Imeldra he was afraid her father might be so severely injured that they would not be skilled enough to attend to him.

"You have notified Dr. Emmerson?" she asked.

"Of course," Mr. Dutton replied. "He was unfortunately out on his rounds, but I am sure by this time the groom will have found him and he should be here at any moment."

Imeldra clasped her hands together.

"Oh, Mr. Dutton . . . how could this . . . have happened to . . . Papa?"

Mr. Dutton shook his head as if he had no words in which to reply.

Then it suddenly struck Imeldra that despite the horror of what had happened, at least her father would not now have to marry somebody he really had no wish to have as his wife.

It was a poor consolation, but she felt that provided he recovered and became his old self again, then perhaps this tragedy was a blessing in disguise.

Even as she thought of it, a footman appeared at the Drawing-Room door to say:

"A carriage is coming down the drive, M'Lady."

* * *

Two hours later Imeldra left her father's bedroom to escort Dr. Emmerson down the staircase to the front door.

"Now don't worry, Lady Imeldra," he said. "Your father, despite the fact that he is not a young man, is extraordinarily strong, and his hard riding and the fact that he has in his own way taken care of his health makes everything far easier."

"You are...sure you can...save Papa's leg?" Imeldra asked in a frightened voice.

"I will do everything in my power to prevent it from being amputated," Dr. Emmerson replied. "Sir George Lawson should be here tomorrow and he is not only an extremely skilled surgeon, but also has a reputation for never using a knife unless it is absolutely necessary."

"I cannot...imagine Papa...crippled," Imeldra said beneath her breath.

The Doctor looked at her and seeing the tears in her eyes said:

"I have always been a very great admirer of your father, and your mother was one of the most lovely ladies I have ever met, not only in looks but in character. I think, since you are a mixture of both of them, you will save your father."

The way he spoke made the tears in Imeldra's eyes overflow and they ran down her cheeks.

"I will try . . . you know I will . . . try," she said in a broken little voice.

"I have known you ever since you were a baby," the Doctor went on, "and I have never known you to lack courage—which is what you are going to need now."

He put his hand on her shoulder as he said:

"It is unnecessary for me to tell you that your father will not be an easy patient, and it will need a great deal of patience to cope with him. But I know you love him, and that is more important than anything else."

He smiled at her, then went down the steps to where his old-fashioned gig drawn by one horse was waiting for him.

Imeldra waved as he drove away, at the same time wiping the tears from her cheeks.

She was just about to go into the house again when she saw a pony-cart coming down the drive and wondered who it could be.

It was obviously not a grand caller, who would have been driving in a carriage with a coachman and a footman on the box.

But the caller, whoever it was, was alone in the pony-cart, and because Imeldra was curious she waited until it had crossed the bridge and was turning into the gravel sweep in front of the house.

It was then she saw that the person driving a well-bred horse and elegant pony-trap was a lady wearing an attractive bonnet edged with a little veil that tied under her chin with pale mauve ribbons.

She wondered who she could be, then thought quickly she had no wish to talk to strangers and it would be best to retreat inside the house.

It was however too late.

The pony-cart was drawn to a standstill and the lady, putting down the reins as the groom who had been holding the head of the Doctor's horse went to hers, waved to Imeldra.

"Who can it be?' she wondered.

Then gave a little exclamation.

She realised it was somebody she had not seen for years, but Beryl Marsden had often come to the house when her mother was alive, and had after her death done everything she could to comfort both her and her father before they went abroad.

Now she ran down the steps to greet Lady Marsden as she got out of the pony-cart.

"Dearest Imeldra!" Lady Marsden exclaimed as she kissed her. "I heard the news of your father's accident in the village and came at once to see if there is anything I can do to help you."

"I suppose it is something that could not be kept a secret," Imeldra said with a stifled little laugh.

"As you can imagine," Lady Marsden replied, "the whole village and I expect everybody on the estate is talking of nothing else. I am so sorry."

Imeldra drew her by the hand into the house and

then into the Drawing-Room, and as Lady Marsden sat down she exclaimed:

"How beautiful you have grown, Imeldra! I always knew you would be as lovely as your mother."

"I wish that was true," Imeldra answered. "But if I look even a little like her I shall be happy."

"You are very like her," Lady Marsden replied. "But tell me about your father. I am only so thankful that he is alive after what I heard was a very bad carriage accident."

Imeldra told her what she had heard from Mr. Dutton and also a little more that she had learned from Danvers, her father's valet, who had returned with him.

However she was very careful not to mention that there was anybody with him when the accident occured, for she knew that it was something they must try to keep from everybody else.

Mr. Dutton had in fact joined her in the Sitting-Room which adjoined her father's bedroom while the Doctor was examining him.

"I have told Jason and the others not to tell anybody that your father was accompanied by a lady at the time of the accident, and that she was killed."

Imeldra looked at him gratefully.

"I am sure that it's what Papa would want. But will they keep silent?"

She knew how much servants talked, and was certain that if they followed their inclination every detail of what had occurred would not only be repeated often, but magnified and exaggerated.

Mr. Dutton's lips tightened.

"I made it clear that the penalty for talking would be instant dismissal," he said. "Since those who were with your father have been employed by him for many years I think it unlikely that they will risk their very comfortable positions here."

"I hope you are right," Imeldra said doubtfully.

She knew that if on top of what her father had suffered already there was to be a public scandal of his running away with a famous beauty like Lady Bullington it would be almost too cruel to contemplate.

"I understand your father was going to Dover," Lady Marsden said now.

"My father was making a short visit to Paris," Imeldra replied, "but now all that matters is to get him . . . well."

There was a little throb in the last word which made Lady Marsden stretch out her hand to take Imeldra's.

"I know what you are feeling, dearest," she said, "and please, let me help you."

Imeldra looked at her in surprise and Lady Marsden said:

"I do not know whether or not you are aware of it, but my husband died two years ago. He was very ill for five years before his death and could not bear anybody to nurse him except me."

It was then that Imeldra remembered that Lady Marsden, whose father had been a neighbour of her father and mother, had married a man very much older than herself.

She also had a vague idea that somebody had told her she had not been very happy.

Looking at her now Imeldra's instinct told her that

she had suffered, and because of it her character which had always been sweet and kind had deepened and become even finer than it had been before.

Thinking back into the past she could remember her mother saying how fond she was of Beryl Sinclair, as she had been then,

She also recalled Beryl's father, who was a very possessive man, had kept her at home and refused to allow her to marry until she was nearly twenty-four.

Then because it suited him he had forced his daughter to accept one of his own contemporaries, and she had little say in the matter.

It occured to Imeldra that for Lady Marsden to come back into her life at this moment was exactly what she needed.

Having seen her father lying unconscious upstairs, looking still exceedingly handsome but with his face very pale and drawn, she was aware it was going to take a long time to get him well again.

It was something she was determined to do, but she was wise enough not to underestimate the magnitude of the task, and was aware that she needed all the help she could get.

"Do you really mean that?" she asked.

"Of course I mean it," Lady Marsden answered, "and you know I will be very tactful and not intrude in any way. If you think I am useless or a bother, you have only to say so."

She spoke quite humbly, and Imeldra impulsively bent forward and kissed her.

"I know if Mama were in my place she would want you," she said, "and I need you very, very much."

Beryl—she refused to allow Imeldra to use her

title—fitted into the household so smoothly and with such charm that even the servants welcomed her.

Danvers sat up with his master at night, and Imeldra and Beryl agreed to take it in turns to be with him continually during the day.

When the laudanum wore off the Earl ran a high fever, and they had to restrain him from moving about and making the wounds on his leg bleed.

His body was also badly bruised and he was in considerable pain all the time.

It was Beryl who suggested that too much laudanum was bad for him and persuaded first Dr. Emmerson, then Sir George Lawson, to agree that he should be given herbs if the pain was unbearable.

It was better, she urged, for him to be clear headed to be able to talk to Imeldra or whoever was with him, even if it involved a little suffering.

"I hate the drugs the doctors give," she said to Imeldra. "They gave my poor husband so many that in the end his brain was affected, and it was impossible for him even to recognize me."

She gave a little sigh before she added:

"When he died I could not help feeling it was a merciful release."

Imeldra gave a cry.

"That must not happen to Papa! You remember how witty and amusing he is. I could not bear it if he became like a vegetable."

"I agree with you," Beryl said, "and that is why we have to keep him from the doctors' drugs. I know only too well the disasters they can cause in the long run."

It was however not very easy, but Beryl not only knew that herbs were efficacious and less dangerous, but she also made some healing salve which helped to cure the wounds on the Earl's leg far quicker than anything the Doctor had prescribed.

"If you ever want a job, Lady Marsden, you can have mine," Dr. Emmerson said jokingly.

But because he was an intelligent and understanding man he was not in the least jealous that Lady Marsden's prescriptions were more effective than his.

At first the Earl was too ill when Imeldra sat with him to talk, but because he had amazing resilience and was, as the Doctor had said, a very strong man, on about the fifth day after coming home he appeared not only to look but to sound more like himself.

Beryl had been with him during the morning, and when he awoke after sleeping for a short while after luncheon, Imeldra was at his side.

He put his hand out towards her and she took it and knelt beside the bed to say:

"Darling Papa! You look better, and my prayers are answered."

"I felt you were praying," the Earl said in a slow voice. "And once or twice, when I came back to sanity from a kind of delirium, I thought you were your mother."

"I am sure Mama was here looking after you."

Imeldra thought there was a faint smile on her father's lips as if he thought the same thing. Then he said:

"Lady Bullington was killed. I hope nobody here is aware of it."

121

"Nobody here knows she was with you, Papa, and Mr. Dutton has sworn all the grooms to secrecy."

Her father gave a little sigh as if of relief before he said:

"Poor woman! It is something which should never have happened."

"It was not your fault, Papa. Everybody has said that."

"I am not thinking of the accident," the Earl said, "but she should not have been with me in the first place."

Imeldra's fingers tightened on his.

"What is done cannot be undone, Papa."

The Earl was trying to recall what had happened. After a silence he said, as if he was talking to himself:

"I told them to take her body to the house of one of her relations who she had told me lived near Dover. The Doctor said he would explain that I had been giving her a lift from London."

He spoke slowly as if it was difficult to put into words exactly what had happened, and Imeldra said:

"That was very clever of you, Papa, and I am sure your instructions were carried out. There has been nothing in the newspapers about the accident."

"That was another thing I was going to ask you," the Earl said. "You are quite sure it has not been reported?"

"No, Papa, and Mr. Dutton has bought all the newspapers since he and I were quite certain it was something you would ask about as soon as you were well enough."

"Good girl!" the Earl said. "I am glad you are here."

He closed his eyes as if his mind was at rest and a few minutes later Imeldra knew he was asleep.

It was impossible when she was sitting with her father not to keep thinking of the Marquis.

Although she was tired when she went to bed she never slept without first praying for him and wondering frantically what she could do to save him.

The more she thought of it, the more impossible the situation appeared.

She remembered how *Madame* Jolie had spoken of papers lodged in her Bank and she was sure she meant a Marriage Certificate and perhaps letters from the previous Marquis which would prove very incriminating.

Unless those papers were destroyed, she could always blackmail the Marquis with the threat of taking her case to the House of Lords.

There she would try to prove that her son André was the rightful heir to the title, the estates and everything else which the Marquis had thought was his.

The more she thought about it, the more incredible it seemed that his father, who had been so respectable, should have committed bigamy, and had never done anything to save his son from the predicament in which he now found himself.

"Oh, darling, how can I help you?" Imeldra asked in the darkness.

She felt as if her thoughts were winging out to him and somehow he would know how much she loved him, how much she longed to see him and to comfort him.

It seemed impossible that they were in fact so close to each other, and yet divided by an impassable barrier, or rather a deep chasm which neither of them could cross.

Sometimes her need for him was a physical agony, and she thought she must ride over to see him, or write to him and ask him to meet her.

Then she knew it would only torture him and he would suffer even worse agonies, just as she would, if it meant having to say goodbye to each other all over again.

She did not need to be told how much he was missing her, and she wondered if he talked to William Gladwin about her, thinking he was her grandfather.

Then she decided the Marquis would find it too painful to talk to anybody and be more likely to keep his feelings to himself.

The only thing she could do was to pray for him, and she sometimes thought that her knees would be worn out by her praying, and that even God was not listening to her.

If He had deserted her, so had her mother, for Imeldra was sure that wherever she might be, her mother would be thinking only of her husband and striving to bring him back to health.

After several days of the arrangement they had made with Danvers, Beryl suggested that he should have a good night's sleep, and that they should take his place at least every third or fourth night.

"Yes, of course," Imeldra agreed. "I should have thought of it myself."

"Your father is not as ill now as he was, and as there is a comfortable sofa in his Sitting-Room, I am sure that whichever of us is on duty can doze there, knowing that we would wake immediately if he called."

"I will take the first watch," Imeldra said.

"Very well," Beryl replied, "but promise that you will wake me at two o'clock."

"I promise," Imeldra answered knowing that Beryl would not allow her to argue.

Because it was much more comfortable to lie on the sofa wearing a nightgown and negligee, Imeldra went to say goodnight to her father with her hair flowing over her shoulders.

He smiled as she went towards him and said:

"You look exactly like your mother when I first saw her with her hair down, and I thought she was the loveliest, most adorable person I had ever seen in my life!"

The way he spoke made Imeldra wish she could hear the Marquis say the same thing to her.

Because he was constantly in her thoughts she sat down on the side of her father's bed and asked:

"Papa, in all your journeyings abroad, did you ever hear of a singer called *Madame* Jolie?"

"Of course I did," the Earl replied, "but I cannot imagine how you have heard of her."

"Somebody was talking about her the other day," Imeldra said vaguely. "What do you know about her?"

"I must have been only twenty when I first saw her in Paris," the Earl said, "and she had just sprung to fame."

"Was she very beautiful?"

"Yes, lovely, quite captivating, and she sang like a nightingale. All Paris had gone mad about her!"

"And you knew her, Papa?"

"I took her out to supper once or twice," the Earl replied, "but she was already in love with an Italian Count, Antonio Celleni."

Imeldra gave a little exclamation.

"But surely I have met him?"

"Yes, of course you have!" the Earl agreed. "Do you not remember when we were in Rome he painted a picture of the Villa in which we were living, and I bought it from him?"

"Yes, of course, I remember him well," Imeldra said.

As she spoke she felt that she could see the Count, a middle-aged man with greying hair and dark, eloquent eyes, telling her how pretty she was and how he would like to paint her portrait.

Although she thought him quite a good artist she had managed to avoid the boredom of having to sit for him when she wished to spend all the time that was possible with her father.

"So *Madame* Jolie was in love with the Count," she said slowly.

"She was not only in love with him," the Earl replied, "but to the horror and consternation of his family, she married him!"

Imeldra was suddenly still.

"She . . . married him . . . Papa?" she managed to say after a moment, her voice sounding strange to her ears.

"It was of course an absurd thing to do from his point of view," the Earl went on, "and I have always been extremely sorry for him. Perhaps that was why I bought several of his pictures which were not particularly good."

"Are you . . . saying that they are . . . still married?" Imeldra asked.

"Of course they are," the Earl replied, "since they

are both of the Catholic faith. But Jolie soon left him because he did not have enough money to keep her in diamonds, let alone in anything else."

Imeldra did not speak and after a moment her father went on:

"Antonio has consoled himself with a great variety of attractive women, but he needed money and a wife with a large dowry, which was what his family had planned for him!"

"I can hardly believe it!" Imeldra exclaimed.

"I wonder what has happened to Jolie now?" the Earl pondered. "For some time she was mistress of the King of the Netherlands, and of a number of other rich men who courted her. I remember one of them, although I do not now recall his name, telling me she was 'one of the sights of Paris.' She certainly made sure that men paid for the privilege of seeing her."

"And all this . . . time she has been . . . married to the . . . Count!" Imeldra said, as if she had to be certain of what her father had told her.

"She certainly is, unless of course she is dead," the Earl replied. "I have not heard of her for a long time."

He spoke casually as if it was of no consequence, but Imeldra's heart was beating tumultuously.

For a moment she contemplated telling her father the whole story. Then she thought it might upset him and it was important for him to be kept as quiet as possible.

"Good night, Papa," she said now bending forward to kiss his cheek. "You know if you want me you have only to call, and I will come to you instantly."

"Thank you, my darling," the Earl replied, "and I feel so much better that I think very shortly that you and that angel Beryl will be able to leave me with just a bell that I can ring, if I need Danvers."

"We will think about it," Imeldra said. "At the same time I like being with you! You are much better, Papa, and that makes me very, very happy."

She knew if she was honest that she was now happy for another reason as well, and when she lay down on the sofa and pulled the blankets over her she was saying over and over again:

"Thank You, God, thank You. You have answered my prayers and now the Marquis too can be as . . . happy as I . . . am."

When Beryl took Imeldra's place at two o'clock the Earl was sound asleep.

"Have a good night," Beryl whispered as Imeldra left her.

But when she went to her own room Imeldra sat down at the writing-table and picked up a pen.

Then she hesitated, wondering how she could tell the Marquis what she had found out.

Her first impulse was to send him a letter, or else ride over and explain what had happened.

Then inevitably a number of difficulties presented themselves: first that although she loved the Marquis and was sure he loved her, it was somehow embarrassing for her to assume that the moment he was free he would wish to marry her.

Although she was sure that they were made for each other, her instinct told her that as a man he must make his own decisions without her forcing them from him.

She knew too that he would have to prove the truth

of the Earl's assertion that *Madame* Jolie and the
Count were married, and it seemed wrong for her to
be standing by him as he did so, almost as if she was
trapping him into marriage.

Everything she was thinking seemed a little mud-
dled in her mind.

At the same time her instinct, which was never
wrong, told her to rush nothing, but to let the Marquis
free himself in his own way, step by step.

She put down her pen and looked at the writing-
paper which she had drawn from the leather box
stamped with her father's crest where it was habitually
kept.

It was engraved with the address and the crest
above it.

She looked at it for a moment before she found a
pair of scissors and cut the address from the top of
the writing-paper.

Then slowly and painstakingly, writing not in her
usual hand but in capital letters, she wrote:

*Madame Jolie was married many years ago to
Count Antonio Cellini, who lives in Rome in his
Villa of the same name, and is well known as
an artist.*

She read what she had written, then placed it in
an envelope with the Marquis's name on it.

She got into bed and lay in the darkness trying to
think how she could get it to him without his being
aware where it had come from.

She knew that once he received it he would be

extremely anxious to learn who had sent him such information, but she did not wish him in any way to connect it with herself.

There was in fact no reason why he should do so, because he had no idea that she had overheard the conversation between himself and *Madame* Jolie.

She knew from the fact that he had not told her the truth, that he would not wish her to know the allegations against his father until the whole miserable story could be refuted and forgotten.

It seemed incredible that *Madame* Jolie should have been able to extort so much money out of him without his making any further enquiries as to whether her story was true, and that he had accepted it at its face value relying on the papers she had shown him.

That they were forged, she now knew, went without saying, but the money the Marquis had given *Madame* Jolie to keep silent amounted to very large sums, even for a rich man.

He must therefore have been very sure that she was speaking the truth if he had believed her without further investigation.

Furthermore he must have convinced himself that to ask questions might make other people suspicious and might inadvertently alert them to what he believed was the truth.

"He was protecting the reputation of his father and mother, not thinking of himself, and I would have done the same," Imeldra told herself. "It is only another proof of how wonderful he is, and how, whatever the sacrifice he had to make personally, he wanted to save his father's good name."

Only to think of the Marquis in such a way made

her love surge over her and she longed for him.

For the first time the darkness and misery that had encompassed her ever since she had left him was lifting, and there was a light at the end of a long, dark tunnel.

'Papa has saved me,' she thought, 'for if he had been killed in the accident, I would never have known the truth about the Marquis and would have lost everything—the two people who really matter to me in my life.'

She said a prayer of gratitude that was so fervent that it brought the tears running down her cheeks, but they were tears of happiness because after such a storm of suffering there was a rainbow in the sky.

chapter six

THE Earl moved restlessly in his bed and after a moment he called:

"Imeldra!"

There was only a little pause before Beryl came to his side.

He looked at her in surprise, then as if remembering how before he went to sleep he had said good night to his daughter he said:

"It must be later than I thought."

"It is nearly three o'clock," Beryl replied in her soft voice. "What can I get you?"

"I would like a drink," he answered, "but I am sorry to have woken you."

"I was not asleep."

She put the candle down by his bed and went to

the table on which Danvers before he had retired had left a jug of lemonade packed with ice.

Beryl poured the Earl a drink and carried it back to him.

He raised himself on his elbow and took the glass from her. As he did so, as if she thought it was awkward for him if she stood over him, Beryl sat down on a chair by the bed.

The Earl looked at her in the candlelight and thought she appeared very young with her fair hair, which was a very different colour from Imeldra's, flowing over the plain blue dressing-gown she wore buttoned to the neck and trimmed with a little row of lace.

"You are not in any pain?" she asked anxiously.

"Very little now," the Earl replied, "except when I move too quickly, and you know the Doctors said that I could get out of bed tomorrow and sit at the window."

"You will soon be riding again and will have no need of your nurses."

He thought there was a slight note of regret in her voice and he replied:

"I have a feeling I shall still need you, apart from being so very grateful to you for keeping Imeldra company. It has meant a great deal to her, and to me, to have you here."

He saw the flush that rose in Beryl's cheeks and she looked away from him because she was shy.

"I was thinking this afternoon," the Earl continued quietly, "that you should not be nursing with a sick old man but should be with your own children."

Beryl gave a little sigh.

"I would have loved to have children," she said, "especially a son, but...my husband was...not a...well man."

The way she stammered over the words revealed to the Earl all too clearly what her marriage had been like.

"You must marry again," he said lightly.

Beryl gave a little laugh.

"I am too old now but I hope when Imeldra marries I may be Godmother to her children."

"When she marries!" the Earl said reflectively. "That is another matter that has been upset by my tiresome accident. Imeldra should be in London enjoying the Season, as I had arranged it for her."

"But you know she would never leave you before you are well enough to do without her," Beryl said, "and I do not think that will be for some time!"

"She is very good to me," the Earl murmured almost as if he spoke to himself, "but she should have the opportunity of meeting the right sort of men."

"I hope she will find somebody to...love."

"So you think love is essential to marriage?"

There was a little pause before Beryl replied as if she had to tell him the truth:

"Yes...there can be no...happiness without it."

The Earl lay back against his pillows looking at her.

"We need not pretend to each other at this hour of the night," he said. "Why did you marry the man your father chose for you?"

Beryl looked startled and he went on:

"Imeldra told me that was what happened and I am curious."

Beryl made a helpless little gesture with her hand.

"There was really no alternative. No-one else had asked for me, and Papa did not like entertaining anybody except his own particular friends of his own age."

"So it was Lord Marsden or nobody."

Beryl nodded. Then she said quickly:

"I should not be . . . talking to you like . . . this."

"Why not?" the Earl asked. "Everybody ought to speak frankly at times, and as I have known you for so many years, Beryl, I might almost be your father."

She laughed.

"You know how old I am! I am thirty-three."

"And I am nearly ten years older."

"To me you have always seemed young," Beryl said, "and nobody could believe you were Imeldra's father!"

"You flatter me," the Earl smiled. "At the same time, I did feel young until this accident."

"You *are* young, and once you are riding again you will feel like your old self."

"I wonder," the Earl said reflectively. "I have an idea that while I have been lying here, I have grown older not so much in my body, but in my mind. I have done a lot of damned silly things in my time, and I might have received a much heavier punishment for them than what I am enduring at the moment."

The Earl was thinking of Lady Bullington and how he had been forced to run away with her, but as Beryl did not know of her existence she merely looked bewildered.

But she knew she must not allow the Earl to feel depressed because he was an invalid and she said quickly:

"I do not think there is anybody who does not admire you for your sportsmanship, and for the high standard you have set in the racing world."

"I would like to think that," the Earl replied, "but there are other worlds in which I do not shine so effectively."

"There is plenty of time for those."

"I hope so," he remarked. "I think when a man gets as near to death as I have been, it makes him wonder what sort of epitaph he deserves when he dies."

Beryl gave a little cry.

"You are not to think of such things or to talk of death! You must look forward to living."

She paused, gave him a shy little smile and added:

"I have always envied you because you had that irresistible *joie de vivre* which the French understand so much better than the British."

"The joy of living," the Earl murmured. "Yes, Beryl, that is true. I have been fortunate enough to enjoy a great deal of my life, but there have also been dark moments, empty ones, and times when I felt very much alone."

"I can understand that," Beryl replied, "but you are fortunate that your intelligence tells you they will not last and that you can surmount them and start enjoying yourself again."

"Is that what I believe?" the Earl asked. "Perhaps you are right. But now we have talked about me, let us talk about you."

Beryl laughed.

"Compared to your adventures my life is just an empty page, a book in which there is very little to read."

The Earl looked at her for a long moment before he said:

"Then it is time you began to live!"

"I do not know how to begin."

"Then that is something we must certainly try to rectify in the future," the Earl said quietly. "It will give me something to plan while I am lying in bed unable to sleep."

"But you must sleep," Beryl protested. "It will help you to grow strong again."

She rose as she spoke and taking his empty glass she put it on the side-table beside the jug of lemonade.

Then she came back to smooth his pillows with an experienced hand.

"As you are restless perhaps you have a temperature."

She put her hand as she spoke on his forehead and her fingers were cool and gentle.

The Earl did not speak and after a moment she said:

"You have no temperature, and I think perhaps you are worrying about something. Let me massage your forehead, and you must try to think beautiful thoughts so that you will fall asleep."

As she spoke she moved her fingers gently over his forehead with a mesmeric movement that made the Earl feel as if she swept away not only his restlessness but the worries which she rightly guessed were at the back of his mind.

Almost before he was aware of it he fell asleep.

*   *   *

Imeldra came back from the garden carrying a large bunch of flowers in her arms.

The lilac was now in bloom, as was the syringa, and she thought she would arrange a vase of them in her father's room which would scent the air and take away the smell of the salves and embrocations with which Danvers massaged his leg.

When she came round the side of the house she saw an impressive looking carriage outside drawn by four horses, a coachman on the box wearing a distinctive green and gold livery, and a footman wearing the same standing by the door.

She looked at it curiously and went up the steps quickly and into the Hall.

"Who is calling?" she asked the Butler in a low voice.

"I've just sent a footman upstairs to find you, M'Lady," he replied, "and to ask if His Lordship's well enough to receive Lord Bullington!"

Imeldra gave a little gasp of dismay. Then she said: "I will speak to His Lordship," and ran up the stairs to enter her father's room.

It was the first day he had been allowed out of bed and he had not dressed but was wearing a dark velvet robe.

Around his neck was a silk handkerchief and it gave him the same dashing, raffish appearance as when he wore a high cravat.

The sunshine was on his face, and although he had

grown very much thinner since he had been in bed, he still looked amazingly handsome and when he smiled at his daughter she thought that no man could be more fascinating.

She closed the door behind her and said in a frightened voice:

"Papa, Lord Bullington is here, and has called to see you."

The Earl stared at her in astonishment before he said:

"Bullington? You are sure?"

"Yes, Papa. But why does he want to see you?"

The Earl's lips tightened, as if he could think of a number of reasons. Then he replied:

"I can hardly be so inhospitable as to send him away. Tell the servants to show him upstairs, and to bring a bottle of champagne here immediately."

Imeldra's lips parted as if she would argue. Then she knew it would do no good.

Of one thing she was sure; that her father was too proud to run away from anything, even a situation which would undoubtedly be an uncomfortable one.

"I will give your orders, Papa," she said.

The footman who had been looking for her was waiting outside the door and she gave him the Earl's instructions.

Then because she was frightened that Lord Bullington would upset her father she was trembling as she went to her bedroom.

The Earl was not trembling, but he was certainly a little apprehensive as he waited for his visitor.

If nothing worse the interview was bound to be

unpleasant, and he knew he was not feeling well enough to endure recriminations or what he suspected would be a desire for revenge which had brought Lord Bullington to Kingsclere.

Because he was determined to face the consequences which he admitted he deserved like a sportsman, he settled himself in a more upright position in the chair. The movement hurt his leg and he winced.

His injured leg was resting on a stool and Imeldra earlier had put over it not a rug which she felt would be too heavy, but a very light shawl.

It had belonged to her mother and she had said as she arranged it:

"This shawl was Mama's, and I feel it will not only keep you warm, but have a healing quality because I know she would want above all things for you to get well quickly."

"That is what I am trying to do," the Earl answered, "and I owe so much to you, dearest, and to Beryl and Danvers who have nursed me so effectively."

"I am glad we have contributed, but I think actually, Papa, it is your indomitable will that has been more effective than anything else. That, at any rate, is what Dr. Emmerson thinks."

"And of course he must be right!" the Earl said mockingly. "Doctors are omniscient—we all know that."

Imeldra laughed.

"Beryl does not think so. She believes it is her magic herbs which have saved you from being drugged and doped that have worked the miracle."

"I must remember to thank Beryl for them."

"I have thanked her already," Imeldra said, "and she keeps thanking me for having her here. I think, Papa, though it is a strange thing to say, that she is happier at the moment than she has ever been in the whole of her life."

The Earl did not reply, but he was thinking about Beryl when Imeldra left him.

The door opened and the Butler announced:

"Lord Bullington, M'Lord!"

The Earl looked at his visitor enquiringly.

Lord Bullington was a tall man with a distinguished presence and a slightly pompous manner.

He was also exceedingly wealthy with an important place in Court Circles, so it was understandable that the very lovely girl who had attracted him the first time he saw her had been eagerly pushed into marriage by her parents.

Elaine Bullington had however admitted to the Earl that she had not been in the least in love with her husband when she married him.

"He was sixteen years older than I was," she had said, "and although it was very exciting immediately the ring was on my finger to become a prominent member of the Social World, it is always rather frightening to live with Lionel."

"In other words you are not in love with him," the Earl had remarked.

"I have never been in love with anybody but you," Lady Bullington had said passionately. "Now I love you, love you until you fill the whole world, and all I want is to be in your arms."

The Earl had been captivated by her beauty, but he had soon found that she was over-demonstrative, and in many ways too passionate to keep him amused.

Since his wife's death he had never been in love with any of the women who entertained him, and he found once the chase was over he became very quickly bored because one love affair was very much like another.

He had never at any time in his affair with Elaine Bullington thought of running away with her, or of making their liaison permanent.

He was in fact, considering how he could bring the episode to an end when Lady Bullington's indiscreet behaviour caused her husband to become aware of what was taking place.

Lord Bullington was an excessively proud man, and he also had a temper which he seldom lost, but when he did it made him act illogically and out of character.

Because he felt so furious, insulted and humiliated by the fact that his wife should prefer any man to him, he had, in a blind rage, threatened divorce proceedings.

It made him consider nothing but his desire to revenge himself on the woman to whom he had given so much, and who he was well aware, if he was truthful, had never given him her heart.

He had sent a Solicitor to call on the Earl to say that he was proceeding with his petition for divorce in the House of Parliament, and he told his wife that she was to move out of his house immediately, and he never wished to see her again.

When, weeping despairingly, Lady Bullington had gone to the Earl for help, he knew there was nothing he could do honourably except take her abroad and wait until she was free before he must marry her.

It was not only something he had no wish to do because of the scandal, but also he was aware that Lady Bullington was not in the least the type of woman he wanted as a wife or a Stepmother for Imeldra.

Too late he had realised he was caught in a trap from which there was no escape, and whatever the cost to himself he must behave like a gentleman.

Now Lord Bullington advanced slowly towards the Earl and only when he stopped a little way from his chair, did he say:

"Good afternoon, Kingsclere! I am glad to see you are better."

"I am still somewhat of a cripple," the Earl replied, "so forgive me for being unable to rise to greet you."

"Of course, of course."

Lord Bullington sat down in a chair near to the Earl and there was an uncomfortable silence until, as if he was aware of the question in the Earl's eyes he said:

"I called to see you, Kingsclere, because I thought it was my duty to thank you."

"To thank me?" the Earl repeated in astonishment.

"I have been told," Lord Bullington went on, "that when you were almost crushed to death you roused yourself sufficiently to have my wife's body sent to the house of her relatives with the explanation that you had given her a lift from London."

Lord Bullington spoke slowly, and now he paused before he added:

"That was a gracious action on your part, and prevented a scandal."

"I hope so," the Earl said quietly, "and may I tell you, Bullington, how extremely sorry I am for being instrumental in causing your wife's death."

"I have heard it was not your fault that the accident occurred," Lord Bullington replied, "but what is important from my point of view is that Elaine, foolish though she often was, was not defamed in dying and there has been no gossip as to why she was driving with you to Dover."

"I hoped after what happened that no-one would know the truth," the Earl said.

"When Elaine's relatives, " Lord Bullington said, "sent a groom to inform me what had happened and how surprised they were, I of course, immediately put the blame on the mail services, explaining that Elaine had written to tell them she was coming to visit them and the letter must have been lost."

"That was clever of you," the Earl remarked.

"I felt it was the only thing to do in the circumstances," Lord Bullington said, "but of course everything was made easy by your action immediately after the accident occurred."

The Earl inclined his head in acknowledgement, feeling there was nothing he could say.

He was relieved when the door opened and the Butler came in with a bottle of champagne and with him a footman bearing crystal cut glasses on a silver salver.

Lord Bullington accepted a glass and quickly drank half of it as if he needed a drink to sustain him.

Only when the servants, having put the champagne in an ice-bucket by the Earl's side, had left the room did he say:

"I have something else to discuss with you, Kings-clere."

"What is that?"

Again Lord Bullington seemed to hesitate over his words, before he said:

"His Majesty, as you doubtless know, is endeavouring to interest himself in horse-racing, a sport of which, having previously been a sailor, he knows very little."

"I have heard that," the Earl agreed.

"The King was asking me," Lord Bullington went on, "to make some suggestions regarding the appointment of a Master of the Horse, and with your permission I would like to put forward your name."

When he finished speaking the Earl stared at him as if he could hardly believe what he had heard.

"Put forward my name?" he repeated.

Lord Bullington took another sip from his glass.

"I am in your debt, Kingsclere. You saved both me and my family a very great deal of unpleasantness and I am prepared to admit that I acted hastily and without due thought. I am grateful to you, and I also think, without prejudice, that you would be an exceedingly good Master of the Horse, if you are prepared to stay in England more often than you have done previously."

The Earl drew in his breath.

"I can hardly believe what I am hearing," he said with a faint smile.

"What I was thinking," Lord Bullington went on as if he had not spoken, "is that it would amuse His Majesty, and certainly be instructive, if you could hold a Horse Show here during the Autumn before the Winter Season starts."

The Earl seemed speechless and he went on:

"I thought a Steeple Chase, or perhaps some competitions for horses of different grades, would be an attraction, and of course Their Majesties would wish to stay at Kingsclere, which the King is well aware is one of the finest houses in England."

If Lord Bullington had exploded a bomb in front of him, the Earl could not have been more surprised.

At the same time his quick mind instantly saw how capably he could organise such an unusual entertainment.

It would certainly be to the advantage of British Racing as a whole that the Monarch was not only interested in what was known as 'The Sport of Kings', but also had a better knowledge of it than he had at the moment.

At the same time it seemed incredible that such a suggestion should come from Lord Bullington.

Then with an air of surprise he heard himself saying:

"It would of course be a great honour to have Their Majesties here, and I quite understand, Bullington, what you are envisaging regarding the horses. As I expect you know, there would be a large number of competitors from this Country, let alone many others!"

"That is what I thought," Lord Bullington replied, "and as Master of the Horse you will have things very much your own way, and can be in London as little or as much as it suits you."

"I can only say that I accept your suggestion with

pleasure," the Earl said, "and I am very grateful."

"As I am grateful to you," Lord Bullington said.

The Earl reached out his hand to the side of his chair and grasped the bottle of champagne by the neck.

"I think, Bullington, it is something we should certainly drink to!"

Lord Bullington held out his glass and the Earl refilled it, then his own.

Shortly afterwards Lord Bullington took his leave, saying as he reached the door:

"Goodbye, Kingsclere. I wish you a quick recovery, and you will doubtless hear from the Lord Chamberlain within a week or so."

"I shall be awaiting my instructions with interest and anticipation," the Earl replied.

The door closed behind Lord Bullington and the Earl leaned back against his pillows.

He knew that never in his wildest dreams would he have expected to have such a conversation with Lord Bullington or to find himself part of the Court Circle.

To be Master of the Horse, he reflected, was the only position at Court that he could accept, knowing that he could carry out his duties more proficiently than anybody else.

Already he was beginning to plan how he would construct a race-course on his estate and build the extra stables which would be needed both permanently and temporarily for the event that would take place in the Autumn.

He had also begun making a list in his mind of those of his neighbours who had the best horses, when Imeldra came into the room.

Looking pale and a little worried she ran to her father's chair saying:

"What happened? What did he want?"

The Earl smiled.

"You will never believe this, my darling," he said, "and I am finding it hard to believe it myself, but you see in front of you the future Master of the Horse to His Majesty, King William 1V!"

Imeldra stared at him.

"What are you saying? What are you telling me?"

"I am telling you, my sweet, that Bullington is advising the King that I am the best man for the job!"

"I cannot . . . believe it!"

"Neither can I, as it happens," the Earl replied. "But we are to have here in the Autumn the largest and most impressive array of horses of all descriptions for His Majesty's inspection, and he with the Queen, will be staying in the house! There is also a race-course to be built in record time, and the sooner we start, the better!"

Imeldra gave a little cry that was half a laugh. Then she put her arms around her father's neck and laid her cheek against his.

"Oh, Papa, it is so wonderful, and exactly what I have wished for you. Now you will not have to go abroad, but you can stay here in England with me."

"Fate certainly works in strange ways," the Earl agreed. "I prevented you by my accident from going to Court, and now the Court is coming to you, my dearest, so why should we complain?"

"Why indeed? Oh, Papa, you will make not only the most handsome, outstanding Master of the Horse there has ever been, but certainly one who knows more about horses than any of your predecessors."

"I hope so," the Earl said, "but one thing is quite certain—I am damned if I will have all those horses here and not be able to ride myself!"

"We will get you well, I promise you we will get you well," Imeldra said. "I must tell Beryl! She will be so excited!"

She turned to walk to the door before the Earl said:

"Yes, tell Beryl, but do not forget—not a word about Lady Bullington."

"No, of course not, Papa," Imeldra agreed, "and I suppose Lord Bullington has suggested this because he is so grateful that there was no scandal."

"I saw to that," the Earl said. "It was fortunate that I could think clearly before the Doctor poured that filthy laudanum down my throat."

"Your old Nurse once said before she died," Imeldra said, "that there was no small boy quicker at getting into mischief than you, and no one so clever at getting out of it again."

The Earl laughed.

"I suppose Nanny was right. At the same time I am glad I have not lost my magic touch."

"So am I," Imeldra said.

She came back to kiss him again.

"Oh, Papa, I am so very, very glad! It is everything I have ever wanted for you, and now we can entertain here and have parties, and it will be just like the old days before you started wandering over the face of Europe."

"Just like the old days," the Earl repeated.

Imeldra knew that he was thinking of how much he would miss her mother, and that however hard she tried, it would not be the same for him as having a wife as hostess to help him.

She ran to Beryl's room and told her what had occurred.

Beryl had gone to bed after being relieved of her attendance on the Earl when Danvers came in to pull back the curtains at eight o'clock.

Although she had dozed for a little while during the night she had been unable to sleep properly in case the Earl should want her again, and she had therefore got into her own bed and slept dreamlessly until her luncheon was brought to her at one o'clock.

Now she was bathed and dressed and was just about to go downstairs when Imeldra burst into her room to tell her the good news.

"Master of the Horse!" Beryl exclaimed. "What could be a more exciting post, and how clever, how very, very clever of His Majesty to think of your father!"

"Yes, it was, was it not?" Imeldra agreed, thinking it best not to mention Lord Bullington's part in it.

Imeldra and Beryl went into the garden and it was not until teatime that they went to the Earl's Sitting-Room to find him giving instructions to the Agent and the Estate Manager.

They were looking a little bewildered as the Earl explained sharply and clearly exactly what he required and the list of orders that both men were taking down as he spoke had already covered several pages of their note-books.

"Papa, you are doing too much, and you have been up far too long," Imeldra said.

Both the Agent and the Manager looked guilty.

"There is lots of time before the Autumn," Imeldra went on, "and now you have to rest, otherwise you will be too ill to entertain your distinguished guests, and the whole thing will be a flop."

"I'm sure you're right, M'Lady," the Agent said. "We'll come back tomorrow, if His Lordship's well enough to see us."

"I shall be well enough," the Earl insisted. "I am just starting to get the plans worked out in detail. I want a full-size race-course, which will mean levelling some of the land at the end of the gallop."

"Yes, of course, M'Lord," the Agent agreed.

Because Imeldra was waiting at the door he hurried through it bowing respectfully to her as he left.

As Imeldra shut the door behind them, Danvers came into the bedroom.

"I'm glad to see you, M'Lady," he said. "His Lordship refuses to listen to me, an' I've been saying for the last two hours he should be back in bed!"

"Well, I am prepared to go now," the Earl said a little wearily. "My head is all right, but my leg is aching."

"I'll see to it, M'Lord."

As Danvers spoke he took the stool away from under the Earl's leg and pushed his chair into the bedroom.

Imeldra brought in the flowers that she had arranged, and as she put them on a table in front of the window she looked out at the Park and wondered whether the Marquis's horses would be competing in the Autumn.

She was sure they would. At the same time, as the days went by after she had sent him the anonymous letter about *Madame* Jolie, she could not help being afraid that perhaps her father's information was wrong.

Supposing that after all the French woman had not actually been married to the Count Celleni, that her son was not his, and that when she had married the Marquis it had been a legal marriage and André was the rightful Marquis of Marizon after all?

Because the questions haunted and taunted her whatever she was doing, Imeldra calculated a thousand times how long it would take the Marquis to journey to Italy, find out the truth, then journey on to Paris to confront *Madame* Jolie.

However quickly he travelled it still seemed to her it must be a century of time before she could see him again.

All she could do was just to send out her thoughts of love and her prayers that he might be saved.

Even to think of him and know they could not be together until everything was settled was still an agony, and even though she believed fervently in her heart that all would be well she felt the tears come into her eyes.

Because she had no wish for her father to know what she was suffering she went to her own bed-room.

A little later Beryl went to find her, expecting her to be with her father.

The Earl had gone back to bed and was sitting up, with the big vases of flowers on either side of him, in the huge red silk-canopied bed in which all the Earls of Kingsclere had slept since the house was first built.

Above his head was the very ornate coat-of-arms

and Beryl thought as she looked at the Earl, that the family motto was very appropriate.

Translated from the Latin, it read: *"I Fight to Win."*

As she walked towards the Earl he lifted his glass as if in a toast to her and she said:

"Nothing could be more appropriate at this moment than the motto above your head."

"That is something I have been thinking myself," the Earl agreed, "and I suppose Imeldra has told you the good news?"

"I am so glad and so very, very happy for you," Beryl said. "I know what a success you will be."

The Earl put down his glass.

"If I am not a success," he said, "I shall not only be a disappointment to myself, but I shall feel I have failed both Imeldra and you."

"I have always thought you should have an important post, not only in the County, but in the Country," Beryl said. "You are somebody people want to follow and admire."

"They can hardly have felt much admiration for me in the last few years," the Earl remarked.

Beryl laughed.

"If you are thinking about your reputation I can assure you that here, while a few old women look down their noses, the men are all both admiring and envious, and the younger ones would give their right arm to be you."

The Earl looked startled.

"Is that true?"

"I promise you it is true," Beryl said. "I have heard them talking about you and all the men of my father's age and my husband's were saying that if they had the chance they would be as dashing, as gallant and as fascinating, while the younger men, although you may not realise it, copy the way you tie your cravats, the way you ride, and count their conquests in the same way they think you do."

Beryl spoke impulsively without thinking, then she blushed at what she had said.

The Earl laughed.

"You certainly surprise me, Beryl. What you have just said is something I never expected to hear."

"It is true, it is really true, and therefore, if what Imeldra tells me is going to happen in the Autumn, it will make everybody polish up not only their horses, but their brains as well as their good manners, and their interest in life."

The Earl put out his hand.

"Come here, Beryl. I want to talk to you."

She moved nearer to him and when she put her fingers in his he felt the little quiver that went through her.

Because he seemed to expect it she sat down on the edge of the mattress facing him, feeling surprised and a little apprehensive of what he was going to say.

"Last night," the Earl said in his deep voice, "you told me you had never been in love. When I thought about it afterwards I came to the conclusion that was not true."

"What...do you...m—mean?" Beryl stammered.

"I think you are in love, but you are afraid to admit it, even to yourself."

She started and would have taken her hand away from his, but he held it closer in his.

"Looking back into the past," the Earl said, "I

think, although I may be mistaken, that when you used to come here when Imeldra was quite young, you were aware of me then, as a man."

The colour flooded into Beryl's face and she looked away from him.

"I thought you were very attractive," the Earl said quietly, "and when I was told you were married, I hoped you would be happy. Now I know that was not so, and because you have come back into my life, Beryl, I hope perhaps I could give you that happiness you have always missed."

There was silence. Then Beryl said in a voice he could hardly hear:

"I . . . do not . . . understand what you are . . . saying to me."

"What I am saying, Beryl, is that I need you, and want you more than I have ever wanted anything in my life. I want you to give me the son you and I have never had, to bring him up here at Kingsclere so that he will be happy in the home that has belonged to his ancestors, and which in time will belong to his children."

Now the Earl felt that Beryl was trembling and her eyes filled with tears as she asked brokenly:

"Are you . . . really saying this to . . . me?"

The Earl smiled in a way that every woman found irresistible as he answered:

"I am asking you to marry me, my darling, and I think, as you need me and I need you, we could be very, very happy together."

Tears ran down Beryl's cheeks.

"I . . . I cannot believe . . . it!" she wept.

The Earl released her hand and put his arms around her to pull her close against him.

"I . . . I have . . . loved you ever since I can . . . remember," she said, "and because I knew you were . . . out of reach and you could never . . . love me it really did not matter what . . . happened to me because I could never . . . love anybody . . . else."

The Earl did not reply. He merely moved her a little closer and his lips found hers.

His kissed her until the rapture he aroused in her was so sweet, so sincere and unspoilt that he knew that this was what he wanted in his wife, and in his home.

"I love you!" he said quietly, "and I swear I will make you happy."

He knew as he spoke that his wandering days were over.

He would settle down and would fill his life with all the things he ought to do in his position, rather than go chasing rainbows which were invariably disappointing.

He was envisaging not only that he and Beryl together could have quite a number of children before she was too old, but that it would bring them a joy which, with his horses, would fill his life, and his raffish, roving days would be forgotten.

His kissed away the tears from Beryl's cheeks and as he did so she said in a voice that seemed to vibrate with joy:

"I love you! I love you, and there is . . . nothing else in the world but you . . . and love!"

chapter seven

"OH, darling Papa! I am so, so glad! It is just what I have wished for you!"

As she spoke Imeldra kissed her father, then Beryl.

"You are quite...certain you do not...mind?" Beryl asked in a soft, anxious voice.

"You are exactly the wife I would have chosen for Papa if he had asked me! I was terrified that he would marry one of those hard, sophisticated beauties who always tried to shoo me away so that they could be with Papa alone."

"You know I would never do that."

Imeldra smiled at her. Then she said to her father:

"Now you must hurry and get well, Papa. There is so much for you to do."

"I know that," the Earl replied in a contented voice,

"and I have not only to make plans for the Horse Show, but also for my marriage."

He looked at Beryl as he spoke and held out his hand.

Imeldra who knew him so well saw that his eyes were kind and tender, and very different from the fiery glances that she had detected between him and the other women since her mother had died.

She had in fact often thought since Beryl had come to Kingsclere how well she fitted in, and how both she and her father would miss her when he was well again and she returned home.

Now it seemed perfect that she could stay on, and Imeldra also knew that if the miracle she was praying for happened and the Marquis wanted her for his wife she would not feel guilty in leaving her father alone.

There was, however, a big question mark as to whether or when that would happen.

She had lain awake night after night thinking of how she could let him know who she was without seeming to push herself onto him or making him feel after all they had said to each other that he was obliged to marry her.

She had seen so many women pursue her father and been aware of how instinctively he had resented their insistence and their demands when he wanted to be free.

Perhaps the Marquis, once he no longer had the menacing mystery of his secret hanging over him, would want to enjoy himself as a bachelor and not immediately be shackled in a new manner.

Imeldra planned, as her father would have, a dozen

different ways in which she could let the Marquis know her real identity without it seeming obvious.

She went over them one after another, feeling somehow in her own mind that as in a fairy story, if he wanted her enough he would find her despite all the difficulties.

Again it was too soon to think about such things.

In her calculations of how long it would take him to get to Italy and back again, she thought it would be at least another three weeks or a month before he could return to England.

Yet it was impossible not to think of him all the time and feel her vibrations going out to him and at times to know irrefutably that he was thinking of her.

"I love him!" she thought now.

She could not help feeling a tiny pang of jealousy when she saw how happy Beryl was with her father.

Because she wished to leave them alone as much as possible, the following day immediately after luncheon she suggested to Beryl that if she was prepared to take over her turn to be with the Earl, she would like to go into the garden to pick some flowers.

"Yes, of course, dearest, I will do anything you want," Beryl replied instantly. "But you are quite sure you really wish to be alone? I cannot bear to think that I am preventing you from being with your adorable father, as you always have been."

"I have never seen him looking so happy or so young," Imeldra answered, "and what is more important than anything else is to keep him feeling like that so that his leg will heal quicker than it would otherwise."

Beryl laughed.

"We are always told that happiness heals the body as well as the mind!"

"That is what we are doing to Papa."

As they left the Dining-Room and Imeldra walked towards the front door, she was aware that Beryl was running swiftly up the stairs, eager to reach the Earl.

It was a warm, sunny day and she did not put on a bonnet, but just walked into the garden as she was, carrying only a basket and the scissors with which she intended to cut the flowers.

As she moved through the bushes of lilac and syringa to a part of the garden which her mother had always kept wild, it seemed almost a crime to take anything so beautiful from its natural place.

In the wild garden there were also a number of magnolia trees in bloom. Their pink and white flowers were opening in the sun, making a picture that was breath-taking in its loveliness.

Imeldra stood looking at them, wishing she could share them with the Marquis.

Everything at Marizon was so perfect that she knew beauty had the same appeal for him as it had for her and aroused a feeling almost like a rapture within her breast.

Because to think of him brought an irrepressible longing to her mind and heart she felt the tears come into her eyes at the very intensity of it, and the magnolia tree at which she was looking suddenly became misty and out of focus.

At that moment she heard footsteps behind her, but because she had no wish for anybody to see her when she was feeling so emotional she did not turn round and only hoped that if it was one of the gardeners, he would pass by without speaking.

Then the footsteps came to a standstill and she thought it might be a servant with a message.

Surreptitiously she wiped her eyes before she turned and as she did so was transfixed.

It was the Marquis who stood there, looking magnificently tall, broad-shouldered and attractive against the blossom, and there was an expression on his face that she had never seen before.

It was impossible to move, impossible to speak.

Then very simply the Marquis held out his arms and with a little cry of sheer joy Imeldra ran towards him and he held her close against him.

She could feel his heart beating against hers before his lips came down to take hers captive, and it seemed as if the sun enveloped them and they were one with the beauty of the flowers.

He kissed her fiercely, passionately, demandingly, and she knew it was not only because he had missed her, but also because he had been afraid of losing her.

Only when a century, it seemed, of wonder had passed in which it was impossible to think of anything but the rapture he aroused in her and the ecstasy that seemed to fill the very air, the Marquis took his lips from hers and she cried incoherently:

"I love . . . you! I love . . . you! But how is it possible that you are . . . here so . . . quickly?"

As she spoke she had a sudden fear in case he had discovered that what her father had told her was untrue, and so had not gone to Italy.

As if he read her thoughts, he merely pulled her closer still and said:

"I am saved, my precious one, and now I can make you mine, as you were always meant to be."

Then he was kissing her again, kissing her with a violence that had a touch of fire in it, and yet Imeldra was not afraid.

She knew that he was making her his own as she had been since the beginning of time, and saying it not with words but with kisses which joined them so that they were no longer two people but one.

Only when they were both breathless did the Marquis say in a voice that was unsteady and curiously hoarse:

"How can you be so beautiful? Far more beautiful than when I last saw you. Then you were already a part of me, and it is not only your face I adore, but every little piece of you which is mine as well."

The way he spoke made Imeldra quiver.

As she hid her face for a moment against his shoulder she managed to ask:

"How...did you...find me? I did not...expect you...back in England...so soon!"

The Marquis laughed and it was a very happy sound.

"When you told me what I should do, I went at once to Paris."

"I told you?" Imeldra exclaimed. "How did you...know that the note was from...me?"

The Marquis looked down at her very tenderly.

"You cannot have forgotten how closely we vibrate to each other, my precious. Do you think I could hold the paper on which you had written, or read the words on it without being aware that they came from you?"

"You were . . . really sure of . . . that?"

"Very, very sure!"

"But . . . you did not know that I had learnt . . . your secret."

The Marquis smiled.

"I did not have to be a detective, my darling, to learn that, and I will tell you all about it. But at the moment all I want to do is to kiss you and ask you how soon you will marry me."

He did not wait for Imeldra to reply, but kissed her until she held him away from her saying:

"I am curious . . . terribly curious . . . and I never . . . dreamt you would come here to find . . . me."

"You underestimate not only my powers of deduction but also my love," the Marquis said reprovingly, "and that is something I will not let you do in the future."

His lips moved for a moment over the softness of her cheek. Then he said:

"When you left Marizon so hurriedly without saying goodbye I could not at first understand what had happened."

"I thought . . . William Gladwin would tell you that . . . my father had had an . . . accident."

"I was told that before I asked the question."

Imeldra looked surprised and the Marquis explained:

"When my visitor left I was so depressed and upset that I wanted to be with you, not to tell you what had occured, but merely to feel the closeness and inspiration you have always given me, besides the reassurance that somehow, in some way I could not at that moment visualize, I would escape from the maze in which I found myself."

Imeldra was listening, but she did not interrupt and he went on:

"I asked the Butler where you were and he replied:

"'Miss Gladwin has left, M'Lord. A carriage came to collect her, and I understand her father has had an accident.'

"'Left?' I repeated, stunned by the information. 'At what time did this happen?'

"'Let me see—' he answered. 'It was, M'Lord, just after Miss Gladwin left the Library where she'd been choosing a book that she went upstairs, and I sent a footman with a note that had just arrived for her with a carriage.'"

"So you guessed," Imeldra said, "that being in the Library I could have . . . overheard what you were . . . saying in the . . . Morning-Room."

"I was sure of it," the Marquis replied, "and I thought at first you had left because you were disgusted and shocked at what you had learnt."

"I was . . . neither of those . . . things," Imeldra answered, "but only terribly worried about you, and wondering desperately how I could . . . save you."

"How could I know that?" the Marquis asked. "I just thought I had lost you."

"I . . . I am sorry," Imeldra whispered contritely.

"I do not think I have ever known such torture as I endured thinking I would never see you again, and yet while my brain told me one thing, my heart was sure that you were thinking of me, and still loving me."

"How could you...imagine I would ever stop...loving you?"

She spoke so intensely with a touch of passion in her voice that the Marquis could only kiss her again.

Only when they both felt the wonder they were experiencing made it impossible for their legs to sustain them did they sit down on a bench beside a magnolia tree, and Imeldra put her head on the Marquis's shoulder while his arms were still around her.

He kissed her hair, then her forehead before he said:

"When I received the note telling me *Madame* Jolie was married to an Italian and knew quite surely that it came from you, it was as if the Heavens opened and a shaft of sunlight swept away the darkness which had encompassed me for so long."

Imeldra looked up at him questioningly.

"So you went to Italy?"

"No, I decided I would start my search in France," the Marquis replied, "because my perception, which you and I both believe in, told me it was the right thing to do."

He kissed her forehead again before he said:

"By then I already knew who you really were."

"How...could you have...known that?"

The Marquis smiled.

"Everybody at Marizon was talking about the accident that had befallen our nearest neighbour, the Earl of Kingsclere."

Imeldra raised her face and the Marquis said:

"You forget, my darling, that I also own racehorses, and since your father's horses invariably beat mine everything that happens to him is of vital interest to my grooms, my trainers, in fact everybody in the house from the Pantry Boy to my Housekeeper, who I believe occasionally 'has a flutter.'"

Imeldra laughed before she said:

"So you all knew that Papa had been involved in an accident!"

"I was very sorry to hear it." the Marquis said, "I also am an admirer of your father."

Imeldra looked at him in surprise, and he said:

"And I love his daughter more than I can ever tell her in words."

He would have kissed her but Imeldra said quickly:

"You have still not explained to me how you found out that I was Papa's daughter."

"It was not very difficult," the Marquis smiled. "I was suspicious Mr. Gladwin was not really your grandfather and when my Agent was telling me that the Earl had had an accident when he was driving to Dover and had been crushed by the impact of the Stage Coach, I said:

"'I am extremely sorry to hear about his Lordship. As his wife is dead, I hope he will have somebody competent to look after him and nurse him back to health.'

"'His daughter's with him, M'Lord,' my Agent replied, 'and I've always heard that Lady Imeldra thinks the world of her father.'"

"So it was as easy as that!" Imeldra exclaimed.

"I could not believe there were many young women in the Country called 'Imeldra,'" the Marquis said, "and besides, when I thought about it, there is a resemblance between you and your father that is ines-capable."

"And knowing . . . who I was you went to . . . France."

"I not only knew who you were, but I was able to guess where the information came from that you had sent me in such a disguised manner."

"What . . . happened?"

"When I reached Paris," the Marquis replied, "I went to see the Head of the *Sureté*, and, my precious, I now know what a fool I was not to have done that very much sooner. It would have saved me a great deal of misery, bitterness and, of course, money."

"What did he say to you?"

"He told me he had been suspicious for a long time that *Madame* Jolie was obtaining money by blackmail in collusion with her brother who had a criminal record as a forger."

The Marquis paused before he added:

"How could I have been so thick headed as not to have investigated her claims before now?"

Because he sounded so self-accusing Imeldra put her arm out protectively to draw him closer to her, and as if he understood what she was feeling he smiled tenderly at her before he said:

"It is all over now! There is no need to go into details. I discovered with the help of the Inspector that Jolie's brother had forged the Marriage Certificate and also the letters, supposedly written by my father, which she had shown me."

"How did she know about him?"

"She had met him once when she sang at a large party at the British Embassy. It was my father's first

169

visit to Paris and he had been given an introduction to the Ambassador by the Foreign Office in England."

He paused before he continued:

"Jolie was very beautiful in those days, and her voice was acclaimed in every country in Europe. Later, in return for so much hospitality, my father decided to give a party of his own and he wrote to Jolie asking her if she would sing at it."

"So she had a sample of his handwriting."

"Exactly, or rather, her brother did."

"And at that time she was married to the Count."

"She had married him three years earlier in Rome and had already run through his money. Their son was actually two years old when she met my father!"

Imeldra gave a deep sigh.

"Oh, darling, if only you had known this before!"

"I know it now," the Marquis said. "I am free, and that is all that matters."

He kissed her and Imeldra said:

"Tell me the...rest of the...story. Then we can...forget it."

"When I confronted Jolie with the Inspector from the *Sureté* and told her that I knew she was married to the Count, she broke down and admitted that she and her brother had concocted the plan of extorting money from me the moment she heard that my father was dead."

"It was cruel," Imeldra murmured.

"She had done the same," the Marquis went on, "with the head of a very distinguished and aristocratic French family, and also a Belgian Baron, who had been paying her for years as I have been fool enough to do."

"It was a very ingenious plan," Imeldra said, "compelling you to protect your family name and your father's memory."

"Of course," the Marquis agreed. "I could not bear to think that my father, who had been the height of propriety and stood in my life for everything that was noble and upright, had deceived my mother by marrying her when he was already married to another woman."

"I can understand what you felt," Imeldra said, "and I suppose that is why you left the fake picture in the Gallery."

"When I first saw you," the Marquis said quietly, "and I was angry because you were saying such disparaging things about me, I thought at the same time, that you were the loveliest, most perfect person I had ever seen."

"Now we can remove the fake and forget it all."

"We will do that," the Marquis agreed. "But I think I shall keep it to remind myself always to have more faith in those I love and to believe not what my brain tells me, but my instinct and my heart."

He gave a deep sigh as if he released the tension within him as he said:

"When I arrived back from France this morning I came straight here to tell your father that however much he needs you, I need you too."

Before she could speak he pulled her close against him to say:

"You gave me hope, my precious, even before you solved my problem, and swept away my despair. You loved me, and inspired me as I beg you to go on doing for the rest of our lives."

"You know that is what I want to do," Imeldra replied, "and, darling, darling, how wonderful it is that you no longer have to feel bitter or resentful."

The Marquis held her closer to him and she whispered:

"You are quite...certain you...really want... me?"

"Do I really have to answer such an absurd question?" he asked. "Although I should really be very angry with you for trying to deceive me, and for not telling me your secret as soon as we knew we loved each other, I suppose I shall have to forgive you."

"I did not...wish you to...think you were...obliged to...marry me," Imeldra said in a low voice.

"I am obliged to do so because I cannot live without you," the Marquis said positively. "And now, let us go and see your father and tell him that however much he wants you, I claim you as mine."

Imeldra laughed.

"A week ago I should have been a little afraid that Papa would be hurt at my leaving him."

The way she spoke made the Marquis look at her questioningly, and he asked:

"But now?"

"Now Papa is going to marry a very old friend, Lady Marsden, and they are so happy together they do not really want me."

"I want you!" the Marquis said, "I want you now, at once! We will be married tomorrow."

Imeldra laughed. Then she said:

"Tomorrow, tonight, whenever you wish! All I want is to be with you, to love you and know I never need feel...lonely again."

The Marquis pulled her almost roughly against him and kissed her until once again the garden, the flowers and the sunshine whirled around them and it was impossible to think of anything but his lips and the wonder of him.

Then he helped her to her feet.

"We have a lot to do together, but first let us go and talk to your father, and then arrange where we shall be married."

"Here, in the Chapel where I was Christened," Imeldra said. "I am sure Papa can be carried down the stairs in his chair so that he can give me away."

"That is exactly what he has to do," the Marquis said, "give you away to me, and once you are mine, my lovely one, I will never let you go. Of that you can be sure."

"I am sure our love is eternal," Imeldra whispered. "We have loved in the past, and we will love in the future . . . but I love you in the present, until you fill the whole world . . . the sky, and there is . . . nothing but . . . you."

The Marquis looked down at her with a tenderness that seemed to transform his face. The lines of cynicism had gone and he looked young and happy.

He had too, Imeldra felt, a radiance that seemed to vibrate around him, and she felt that he was seeing her in the same way and that their love was a living force which came from them both and was a power which they could never lose.

"I adore and worship you," the Marquis said in his deep voice. "You are what I have sought for all through the years, and thought I would never find! Now I know I have been blessed as few men are, and

I am eternally and humbly grateful."

Imeldra's eyes were on his and as if she could not help it she lifted her arms and put them around his neck and drew his head down to hers.

"We have found the path through the maze together," she said, "and now there are no mysteries, no threats, no evil . . . only love."

The Marquis's lips would have touched hers, but she said:

"Teach me to love you as you want to be loved and we will make Marizon a place of happiness not only for ourselves . . . and our . . . children but for . . . everybody who . . . knows us."

She knew her words touched the Marquis by the way his arms tightened.

Then as he kissed her there was not only the fire that had been there before, but also something ecstatic and spiritual as if what they felt for each other was not only human, but divine.

Imeldra knew this was the real love that her father and mother had known and which she had been afraid she would never find.

The Marquis was a part of her as she was a part of him and, as she had said, there was no more fear or despair, but only a love which would grow, and which would radiate out from both of them to help other people.

"I love you! I love you!" she said because there were no other words in which to express her feelings.

"And I love you! You are mine, Imeldra, for ever and for ever!" the Marquis replied.

Then there was only the sunshine, the scent of the

magnolias and the vibrations of love which seemed like music, and filled the whole garden with an incredible ecstasy.

*　　*　　*

The Marquis and Marchioness of Marizon walked arm-in-arm through the trees towards the sea.

It was a deep blue shading to emerald, and as there was no wind there was only a slight swell which broke very softly below the cliffs on the golden sands.

The sunshine seemed dazzling and the horizon shimmered in a haze.

Imeldra put her head against her husband's shoulder and said:

"It is so beautiful! How could you possess anything so lovely and neglect it for so long?"

"I think I was waiting to come here with you," the Marquis replied. "My mother was left this house when her father died, but I thought it would not interest me to be here alone feeling, as you know, bitter and resentful because I believed my father had deceived her."

"But all the time it was here . . . a perfect honeymoon . . . place for us . . . both."

"Do you find it perfect?" the Marquis asked.

She smiled up at him and he thought he had never seen a woman look so radiant or so happy.

"Ever since we have been here," she answered, "I have felt enchanted. Every night I go to bed thinking it would be impossible to love you more than I do already, only to wake every morning and know that

I not only love you more, but am so wildly, ecstatically happy that I think we must be in Heaven, and not on earth."

"That is how I feel too," the Marquis replied. "Oh, my precious, there is so much for us to do together, so many things I want to show you, and you to show me. But first we are both learning about love, and that is more enthralling than anything else in the whole world."

"It is all that and so much . . . more."

Because she loved the Marquis so overwhelmingly Imeldra lifted her face to his and he kissed her until she felt the fire on his lips arouse an answering flame within her breast.

There was no need for words. The Marquis turned her away from the sea and they walked back through the shadows of the trees towards the beautiful low-built, white-stone house which stood in a sheltered garden and which, as Imeldra had said, seemed enchanted.

It was filled with many things which the Marquis's mother had treasured, and most of all portraits of him from the time he was a baby until he was a young man.

After the grandeur of Marizon it was cosy and intimate, and as Imeldra had said, was a perfect place for a honeymoon because they seemed isolated here in a tiny world of their own in which nothing unpleasant could encroach.

The whole place seemed to radiate with happiness, and she knew that she had never been a complete person until she had met the Marquis.

He not only aroused her body but her brain, and

sharpened her instinct and her perception as she did his.

Every day they discovered new and exciting things about each other, and every day and night, as Imeldra had said, they fell deeper and deeper in love.

Now as they reached the house not talking but communicating without words, Imeldra turned her head for a second to glance at the Marquis questioningly and as she met his eyes she knew what he wanted.

Slowly, still close, they went up the pretty curved staircase which led to the first floor, into a room with two bay windows through which could be seen a vision of trees and the blue of the sea.

But as the Marquis shut the door behind them Imeldra had eyes only for him and he said:

"I think it is time, my darling, adorable wife, for you to rest, and as I have every intention of resting with you, let us make ourselves more comfortable."

He pulled off his elegant cutaway coat as he spoke and threw it down casually on a chair.

Then he put his arms around her, and with his lips on hers he began to undo the buttons at the back of her gown.

When he was planning their honeymoon he had told her that, while he intended to take with them several of his oldest servants from Marizon, he would not allow her to have a lady's maid.

"I intend to look after you myself, my lovely one," he had said, "and a maid fussing round you will only be a nuisance."

"It will give you a great deal to do," Imeldra teased.

"You will find I am very experienced."

"Now you are making me jealous," she protested.

"There is no need for you to be," he answered. "If I have ever known any other women in the past, it is impossible now to remember even their names, their faces, or if they ever meant anything to me."

"And shall I be . . . sufficient for you in the . . . future?"

"If you doubt that," he replied, "then I must prove it to you, not in words, but in a very much easier way."

Now as his fingers released her gown and it slipped to the floor, he lifted her in his arms and Imeldra felt the wild excitement he always evoked in her rising up from her breast into her throat.

She wanted his kisses, the touch of his hand and for him to love her.

He laid her on the bed and pulled the sheet over her, then a few seconds later when he joined her, she knew that the music she had heard in the Temple when he had first kissed her and which was singing in the air around them, also came from themselves.

The Marquis's arms held her, his face was very near to hers, but he did not kiss her, he only looked at her and asked:

"What is it about you that is so different from anybody else? So lovely that you are part of the sea, the sky and the flowers, and yet you are more beautiful than all of them?"

"That is what I want you to think," Imeldra whispered. "At the same time my world contains everything here and all the beauty we have known and taken into ourselves. I think you said once that love is beauty, and that, my wonderful husband, is why I want to be beautiful for you."

"You are beautiful!" the Marquis answered. "So incredibly, unbelievably beautiful that you fill my whole life with a glory that I know comes from God."

"How can you say such marvellous things to me?" Imeldra asked. "That is the love I want to give you, and one day we will both . . . give it to our . . . children."

The Marquis pulled her closer to him.

"I want more than I can say in words you to give me a son, my beautiful wife. At the same time I shall be very jealous if you love our children more than you love me."

Imeldra laughed.

"Do you think that would be possible? We will love them and never leave them lonely or lost. At the same time, you will always be first, very, very, much . . . first, in my mind . . . my heart, and of course . . . my soul."

"Can I possess them all?"

"Everything that is me, and I have nothing else of any . . . importance to . . . give you."

"There is nothing else I want."

Then he was kissing her insistently, demandingly but at the same time tenderly, as if he was afraid to hurt her.

Because it was different Imeldra felt her whole being respond to the rapture of it, and she knew that once again her love had increased and was greater than it had been before, either yesterday, this morning, or a few moments ago.

It was like the ceaseless roll of the waves moving eternally, and their love, as the Marquis had said, was not only human, but divine.

Because she could feel not only love, but a rising

excitement from the fire on his lips, the touch of his hands and the closeness of his body, Imeldra moved even closer to him.

"Love me . . . love me! Oh, my dearest . . . I want your . . . love!"

"As I want you," the Marquis said, and his voice was deep and passionate. "You are my heart, my soul, and my life, my lovely one but you are also a woman. My woman! Mine!"

"Love me . . . love me . . ." Imeldra begged.

Then the music around them seemed to sweep away the sound of their voices, the waves came from the sea, and the fragrance of the flowers surrounded them.

As the Marquis carried Imeldra on the wings of ecstasy towards the sun, there was only love . . . and love . . . and love.

181

Miss Cartland in 1978 sang an Album of Love Songs with the Royal Philharmonic Orchestra.

In 1976 by writing twenty-one books, she broke the world record and has continued for the following five years with twenty-four, twenty, twenty-three, twenty-four and twenty-three. She is in the *Guinness Book of Records* as the best selling author in the world.

She is unique in that she was one and two in the Dalton List of Best Sellers, and one week had four books in the top twenty.

In private life Barbara Cartland, who is a Dame of the Order of St. John of Jerusalem, Chairman of the St. John Council in Hertfordshire and Deputy President of the St. John Ambulance Brigade, has also fought for better conditions and salaries for Midwives and Nurses.

Barbara Cartland is deeply interested in Vitamin Therapy and is President of the British National Association for Health. Her book *The Magic of Honey* has sold throughout the world and is translated into many languages. Her designs "Decorating with Love" are being sold all over the USA, and the National Home Fashions League made her in 1981 "Achiever of the Year."

Camfield Romances by

BARBARA CARTLAND

Called after her own beloved Camfield
Place, each Camfield Romance by Barbara
Cartland is a thrilling, never-before
published love story by the greatest
romance writer of all time!

_____06293-6 THE POOR GOVERNESS #1	$1.95
_____06294-4 WINGED VICTORY #2	$1.95
_____06292-8 LUCKY IN LOVE #3	$1.95